Enough Really is Enough

VIVIEN HEIM

Ordering Information:

BookTrail Agency
8838 Sleepy Hollow Rd.
Kansas City, MO 64114

This book is dedicated to
the memory of my dear parents
who inspired my love of a good story

Acknowledgements

I can't begin to thank so many people enough – for their help, encouragement, support, downright nagging – and even gentle cynicism on occasions. However, I must make some special mentions.

To my daughter Harriet, who's been cheering me on from the side-lines throughout, for making me sit through a photoshoot and for all the times she told me to never give up.

To Audrey, who never stopped believing in me.

To everyone at hostelries and cafés various in Stratford upon Avon, all of whom have been unendingly wonderful to me – supplying me with tea, coffee, lots of laughs and vibrant places to write.

To patient friends/proof-readers, without whom this book probably would never have seen the light of day. So, huge thanks to Penny Calvert, Ric Dubois, Susan Hart, Rod Innes, and Julie Mayall.

To the Book Trail Agency who have held my hand during the publishing process, giving unstinting support and reassurance throughout.

And finally, to you – my readers. Thank you for reading this, my debut novel. Enjoy...

Introduction

I was slowly drifting in and out of consciousness, hazy moments suspended between sleeping and wakefulness when reality slowly nudges into an awareness of what's really happening. For me, that delicious state was usually the stuff of dreamy relaxation, tantalising fantasy, or simply indolent planning – but not this time. This time, taking the tiniest of shallow breaths was a hugely painful effort and the rising sour taste of bile made me swallow hard as I fought the urge to actually throw up.

And then, from far, far away I thought I heard my name. "Lucie... Lucie?" The voice was irritatingly real but I so wished it would shut up, desperate as I was to slide back into pain-free oblivion. "Lucie? Wake up sweetheart, that's a good girl..." Girl? Who the hell was calling me a girl? And me just shy of my 67th birthday. Automatically, the corners of my lips moved upwards very slightly. I heard the voice again. "She's coming round. At last..." Making a superhuman effort I opened my eyes to see two faces looking down at me; despite the fact they were both wearing masks, it was clear that, for some reason, they were more than a bit concerned. It was all too much; I closed my eyes again. "No Lucie, wake up. You've got to wake up…" They sounded quite insistent, so I obeyed – this time, to my immense relief, looking up felt a little easier.

It took what seemed an awful long time to remember where I was and why I was lying on a hard, flat bed in what I saw was a recovery room, after a surgery I'd been desperately trying to ignore. Heaven knows why I'd been so afraid – after all, it was just a procedure that so many before me had undergone, but I'd been utterly terrified as I lost consciousness however many hours ago I'd drifted into drug-induced oblivion. Looking down at myself, I saw a canula in my left hand which deterred much movement; along with spiders, needles had always been one of my phobias. I tried to flex my hand but quickly realised doing so really hurt, my other hand was free though so I managed to raise it but the effort was all too much so I dropped it again. I closed my eyes as full awareness of what had happened whilst I was unconscious sunk in, and felt tears squeezing out from under my closed eyelids. Even the act of crying hurt though, so I lay still and tried to take a few deeper breaths.

About twenty minutes later I was feeling better. I'd coped with being propped up and was drinking a glass of tepid water that tasted strangely musty. "It's because you've had tubes down your throat," was the explanation when I'd wrinkled my nose at the first sip. Shortly afterwards I was back in a side-ward, dimly hearing the soft slapping sound of footsteps and murmured conversations. Despite being told in a voice I'd so often used in my own working life that I really should try to stay awake, I simply couldn't – my eyelids became heavier and heavier and, as I drifted into uneasy drowsiness, memories of what brought me to this place crowded in...

Chapter 1

Richard had been adamant that he was way too busy to drive up earlier (I wasn't too clear as to exactly why he couldn't have done what needed doing at his when he'd had all week, but his explanation had seemed perfectly plausible when we'd discussed it) so he was due to arrive early evening in time for dinner. I was all too well aware that food shopping wasn't high on Richard's nice-to-do list and always tried to make sure that chore was over and done with before he arrived, so had been out bright and early that morning. Now it was Saturday afternoon. Much to my satisfaction, the house sparkled and shone although I'd not bothered to do much in the garden but very often, bless him, Richard would tidy things up out there. And I was wearing a dress – Richard much preferred me fully made up and in girlie clothes. My weekday makeup was usually kept to a swipe of eye pencil plus a dash of bright lipstick, and I normally wore jeans or, on a day when I wanted real comfort, leggings, but knowing his penchant for a more 50s look I usually obliged.

I was comfortably settled in my favourite chair with a mug of tea, doing the crossword when the phone rang which startled both cats who were happily snoozing at each end of the sofa.

"Hi, it's Carrie. Fancy a catchup coffee? Or are you busy with lover boy?" Her voice was slightly mocking; she'd never liked Richard, and certainly not since they'd had a heated argument about... it was now so long ago I couldn't even remember what it had been about but ever since then, both had steadfastly refused to talk to each other. That was such a pity, Carrie was one of my dearest friends. I'd so wanted Richard to get on with all my friends but too many of them for comfort had said, very politely of course, that they'd much rather see me without him. At first that had hurt a great deal, but by now I was used to having the weekdays to socialise with people with who were important to me, keeping the weekends for just the two of us.

'No, no, he's not here yet... yes, I'd love to – when's good for you?' We agreed to meet at the Boathouse which was almost close enough for me to call it my local. Given its amazing views over the river, wonderfully welcoming staff and excellent menu it had been one of my favourite watering holes in Stratford upon Avon for many years. As the rain was pelting down, I decided to drive with fingers crossed there'd be a space in the pub's tiny carpark and, as I did so, reflected on Richard's and my relationship.

I'd lost the love of my life, my wonderful husband Alex, in a dreadful multi-car accident nearly fifteen years previously. He'd valiantly fought for life but after several weeks I'd been forced to admit he was never going to recover and agreed to have his ventilator switched off, a decision that still occasionally haunted me in guilty nightmares. Terrifyingly, I'd been left with crippling money problems so had had to sell our lovely home which was heavily mortgaged, but was lucky enough to raise just enough equity to put a tiny deposit on something very much smaller. Along with the trauma of all that, I'd had to cope with Susie, our ten-year-old daughter (she'd made her surprise appearance several years after we'd come to terms that we were unlikely to have children) who not only took her father's death terribly hard but, of course, didn't really understand, or indeed want to understand, why we had to move. Tricky times indeed but somehow, with lots of love and support from very dear friends, I coped. We'd scarcely found our feet when I was made redundant a year or so later. Still, I had my teacher's pension and that, with a few bits and bobs of teaching, coaching, training and invigilation work from various sources, enabled me to keep my nose above water – just. It was all a bit brinkmanship which made survival a real challenge sometimes but, one way or another, things seemed to work out even if it was quite hair-raising from time to time.

Saying Susie was difficult after her father's death was a huge understatement but, goodness knows how, we'd managed to weather the many crashing lows. Even though she hated school, through a blend of my angry shouting, tearfully pleading, and coldly threatening, she stayed on for her A-levels before flouncing out all the way to Brighton to enthusiastically embrace drugs, sex, and rock and roll. And then, as I was deepest despair about how her life was turning out, she suddenly announced she was going to university as a mature student; the word 'mature' made me smile but it was clear that she was absolutely serious, opting to study engineering. It was during that time, much to my delight, we made friends again. After that she'd spent a year's internship at Fiat's head office in Italy's beautiful Turin; truly her father's daughter in that she was a real petrol-head.

I'd spent ten glorious days with her the previous summer and so envied her Italian lifestyle, not to mention the beautifully balmy weather. After Fiat, she'd been lucky enough to secure a two-year contract with Alfa Romeo. I strongly suspected another pull on her wanting to stay was her new boyfriend, Patrizio. I'd only met him the once but could see and feel the palpable sparks between them. He was as dark-haired as she was blonde, with soulful brown eyes that, most of the time, were gazing into her baby-blues; an altogether appealing and kind-hearted young man who I'd instantly warmed to. I was very happy she was with someone I felt her father would have heartily approved of, when I told her this, we both cried tears of sentimental joy mingled with true hopes for a joyful future. It was heart-warmingly wonderful to be so close to her again.

But the house was eerily quiet when she'd gone which, and for the first time in a long while, gave me the time and space to consider what I wanted rather than Susie being foremost in my mind. More and more it felt like it was my time now. For many years the thought of another man in my life had seemed disloyal to Alex's memory and what we'd had – treacherous even – but I did wonder if I might be lucky enough to find another Prince Charming, chances were not but one never knew. What I did know was that whilst I was very happy in my own space, the thought of having a 'significant other' in my life was increasingly tempting.

After some gentle urging by my girlfriends, I'd gingerly posted my profile onto a well-known dating website. To my delighted surprise I had great fun – flirting, chatting and even meeting a few men but no-one ignited any sort of spark. I'd almost given up when a nice-looking man called Richard winked at me so, as I rather liked the look of him, we messaged a couple of times before meeting. When asked where we should meet, naturally I suggested the Boathouse, in fact that was where I'd suggested to all my dates so the staff were well used to seeing me there with different men; by the time I met Richard they were giving each chap marks out of ten that both they and I found very entertaining. I had to say his photograph didn't do him justice – he was good-looking, tall, clean-shaved, his thinning grey hair worn just a little too short for my liking, and immaculately dressed in highly-polished dark tan shoes, black jeans, and a blouson-style black leather jacket under which was a snowy white tee-shirt. His cologne reminded me of woods and outdoor autumnal walks but, if I was being brutally honest, had been applied a little too generously. However, his piercing blue eyes, sardonic smile, interesting conversation and occasionally off-beat sense of humour made me melt within minutes. There was clearly a mutual attraction on that first date so I was more than happy to agree to a second, but what really bowled me over was the deluge of daily emails, it had been a very long time since I'd been wooed so ardently. I loved the novelty of having a 'boyfriend' although that word seemed very odd at my age. So, despite living about seventy miles apart, we'd now been seeing each other most weekends for close on five years.

Inevitably there were a few glitches along the way. I loved hand-holding while walking but he hated that so we didn't. An enthusiastic foodie I loved talking about recipes but that wasn't one of his interests so we didn't. I loved socialising with my friends but, more often than not, he was awkward with them so we didn't. However, he assured me he 'liked' me a lot, and we spent many happy hours walking, window shopping, going to pubs, the theatre, outdoor concerts and so on, so the positives, certainly at the beginning, far outweighed the negatives. One thing we enthusiastically agreed on was bed, he was into sex which I adored – initially. Gradually, what I came to realise was that while he was indeed sexy, lingering sensuality wasn't really his thing – when I gently raised the subject, it was laughingly rebuffed in such a way that I felt I was being unreasonably demanding. But, on the whole we got on more than we didn't and, I told myself, maybe at my age that was as good as it was going to get.

The gods must have been smiling on me because someone was leaving just as I arrived. Waving an enthusiastic 'thank you' to the departing driver, I manoeuvred into the slightly cramped space which meant I had to squeeze out sideways. Carrie had managed to bag a table and, as I pushed my way through the noisy crowds, I saw an elegant hand waving enthusiastically and joined her. She looked terrific; her slender legs meant jeans always looked fabulous on her and, as usual, she was wearing her 'lucky' pink sapphire ring which had caught my eye under the lights. I could tell she'd recently gone to the hairdresser; her shoulder-length blonde hair was now streaked with pale highlights – come the autumn she favoured slightly darker, auburn lowlights which looked equally good on her. She knew I'd always been a bit of a lightweight alcohol-wise, so had ordered me a small dry white wine spritzer over ice. We'd vaguely known each other for some thirty years when we'd worked together for a short time, and been firm friends ever since our girls had sung in the same choir. She was caring and supportive – we'd seen each other through husbands, divorces, bereavement, jobs, kids and, in her case, more than one lover – I'd long admired her romantic goings-on. The cornerstone of our relationship was a searing honesty which sometimes hurt but was always, always well meant. As was so often the case, after telling each other about our respective weeks, we ended up discussing men.

Fairly recently Carrie had started dating Jake, a local artist. Ever the cougar, she'd discovered he was over twenty years her junior but they got on well and, as she joyously said, life with him was never dull. Despite his flirtatious ways, he was the one who was pushing for them to live together and it was Carrie who steadfastly refused. "I like my own space," she'd said to me more than once; given that she was much involved with both her grown-up children who lived locally and had families of their own, I could well see what she meant.

But for me? Five years on Richard was still more than happy with our weekends-only relationship punctuated with the odd weekday telephone call. Initially it'd suited me very well too but, after the first couple of years, to my slightly disbelieving surprise, I found myself wanting more. More time, more sharing, more of our lives being truly intertwined, much more commitment – but on the rare occasions I tentatively raised the subject Richard made it abundantly clear that our 'modus operandi' as he called it, suited him just fine. And the reasons he gave sounded so sensible at the time that I found myself agreeing with him; it was only later when I'd had enough time to mull things over that I realised absolutely everything he'd said had been entirely practical; my – not to mention his – emotions really hadn't been acknowledged at all. The other thing that occasionally bothered me was that on the few occasions we'd spent time at his, he'd seemed far less relaxed, making it abundantly clear he'd much rather be in Stratford. But equally I had to admit that a part-time relationship really wasn't such a bad thing in some ways – did I really want to live full-time with someone, dirty socks and all? It was then that I'd shrug impatiently and tell myself that I had the best of both worlds even though, deep down, I knew that was exactly what I wanted.

A couple of hours later, I was back home and starting to prep dinner – a pork tenderloin and chorizo cassoulet. I took down my favourite Le Crueset pan, my love of cooking meant I'd treated myself to a few very expensive pots and pans over the years and always enjoyed using them. As I watched the contents of the pan become red with the paprika-y oils from the chorizo before adding slivers of red peppers, garlic and onion along with chunks of tenderloin pork followed by tins of borlotti beans and tomatoes, I pondered on what Carrie and I had been discussing.

As so often was the case, she was quite right. Richard and I had slid into what seemed like this rather banal family-life awfully quickly with many of our weekends following an all too predictable pattern. And for some time that had been okay; after all I had freelance work which I found both stimulating and rewarding, I had lots of interests and of course my friends, so by the weekend I'd been very happy to chill. And, certainly at first, Richard was a caring, considerate man who made an effort, occasionally surprising me with little outings and treats, who made me laugh, and who, despite his aversion to talking about his feelings, had shown a degree of tenderness and affection. Not like Alex of course – but then, no-one could, could they?

I sighed crossly at myself and wondered why he found talking about our future so hard.

Alex and I had always shared everything however difficult or painful, so I'd been used to a man who always did his best to listen and appreciate my point of view. He certainly always put 'us' first. He'd loved me openly and was as honest as the day was long. A man who was, as I liked to put it, emotionally naked; to me an incredibly beguiling masculine trait – unfortunately not one that Richard had shown that much of. And whilst I knew there could never be another Alex, for sure there must be some men who were prepared to get at least half-naked emotionally and that would probably have to be enough.

I absolutely knew Richard cared for me even though he could never bring himself to utter what to me was that all important word, 'love'. Equally, I cared for him – I was more than happy to say it was love, but his continued reticence made me increasingly wary. The last thing I wanted to do was force him into saying what he didn't mean or make a decision he didn't want to make but I so wanted a proper acknowledgement of what I meant to him. His 'Don't be so silly babe, I'm here, aren't I?' was beginning to wear thin.

A little later Richard arrived. We hugged warmly and after a restorative drink, he pulled out my old battered red-and-gold leather footstool that Alex and I had bought one unforgettable holiday in Egypt, put his feet up, leaned back and closed his eyes. I sat in an adjacent chair and gazed at his tall, lean frame, silver hair and chiselled features. There was absolutely no doubt about it, he was handsome and even in repose and after all these years, he was still pretty fanciable.

Our time together hadn't lessened his preoccupation in how he looked, all too often taking much longer than me when getting ready to go out. I remembered that once as I was applying my makeup, he'd taken a shower and then come into my room, stood naked in front of the mirror and flexed his muscles. "You lucky, lucky girl." I'd looked at his hard, lean body appreciatively, for a man in his late sixties there was no doubt he was in amazing shape but after throwing a pillow at him and telling him to hurry up, it had struck me that whilst it was meant as a tease, deep down he'd really meant it. I was the lucky one in this relationship, not him.

One thing he found very difficult to come to terms with was his thinning hair, spending much time and money in products to hold back the inevitabilities of his genes, his father had lost most of his hair in his forties – I'd quickly learned not to comment on this very sensitive subject.

After about half an hour he opened his eyes, yawned and stretched. "That's much better." He smiled. "I'm starving. Shall we eat?"

He opened the fresh bottle of Southern Comfort, his favourite drink, which I always made sure was in plentiful supply, and poured himself a large glass. He laid the table, forgetting to put out the paper napkins as usual. I lit the chunky candles that were on the table.

He grinned at me. "What is it with you women and your bloody candles?"

"They add atmosphere – and romance." I meant it too.

He snorted. "Romance? Hmmm... don't you mean sex?"

"No, I mean romance," I retorted. "Stop being an old grouch, and here..." I passed him two napkins, blue to match the candles. He grinned as he raised his eyes heavenwards.

After dinner I replenished our empty glasses, picked up a large box of chocolates I'd bought just because I'd fancied them, and tucked it under my arm. As I joined him in the sitting room, he looked at it and then up at me. "Well, that diet didn't last long, did it?" Silently I passed Richard his glass as he took the box from my outstretched hand, tore off the wrapper and popped a large nut cluster into his mouth.

I could feel my face getting hot. I'd been about fifteen pounds or so lighter when we first met, but still on the curvy side. Richard had made it very clear very early on that he really liked his women to be curvaceous. When I heard this, I could hardly believe my luck. Here was a man who revelled in voluptuous women – lumps, bumps and all. We'd spent many happy times in various restaurants sampling all kinds of dishes so, it was inevitable I gained weight. As my jeans and shirts got tighter, Richard started to criticise my ampleness, yet in bed he delighted in my body. Such mixed messages I reflected, as my clothes became snugger and snugger and during the weeks I continued to struggle with diet after diet.

"Don't be mean. They're my favourites. And you like them too." I took a salted caramel and ate it with relish even though I knew deep down that, infuriatingly, he was quite right. He didn't answer as he took a second chocolate while, smilingly, he looked me up and down.

Good-looking he certainly was with a bewitching smile he often used to good effect but, more often than I'd have liked, his sense of humour could verge on the spiteful.

A little later we cuddled on the sofa together, watching a horror movie, not my choice but they were one of Richard's favourite genres.

I was dozing off when I felt him gently caressing my breast. As my back involuntarily arched and my nipple hardened, he laughed softly. "Hmmm... time for bed?"

"Why not here?"

"You know I'd rather be comfortable, don't you?" In the past I'd occasionally suggested making out in different locations, indoors or outside, but every time his answer had been that he much preferred the comfort of bed, which meant our love-making was usually confined to night-times.

He stood, reached down and pulled me to my feet. Still holding my hands, he took a step towards to the door, gently pulling me with him.

Richard always used the small spare room as his dressing room so disappeared to get ready for bed. As I undressed and pulled on my short satiny coffee-and-cream-polka-dot nightdress and went to the bathroom, I felt my arousal fading. By the time I'd slid into bed, hearing Richard in the bathroom, it had vanished completely.

Moments later he joined me. "Now where were we…" His hands reached for me and I automatically moved into his tight embrace. We'd been together for nearly five years so perhaps it was inevitable that there would be a certain predictability in bed.

The fact my sex-life with Alex had never been unexciting or monotonous, even after Susie was born, seemed to have escaped my memory.

As we kissed, nibbled and stroked each other we gazed into each other's eyes. I could see his urgency rising and closed my eyes, trying to get into the moment but, as had been happening more often, I faked it. Throwing back my head, I gasped, moaned and clung to him as we fucked rhythmically, moving inexorably towards orgasm. To my surprised delight I felt my own desire mounting until, suddenly, with a soft groan he came, and collapsed over me.

Laying in exasperated frustration, I felt him roll off me and get himself comfortable for sleep.

I stared at his profile for a few moments, then turned onto my side. "Mmmm… that was nice." He patted my hip, his breathing deepening into light little snores. It took me some time to get to sleep.

The next morning, Richard went for a run while I started to prepare us a full English breakfast. On his return, he decided to prepare the grate, ready for that evening's fire, the days were mainly warm but the nights decidedly chilly. "You do so much for me, I just want to help." I smiled fondly at his words. He went through to the sitting room. "Could I have a bag for the ashes please?" His voice floated through.

I sighed, stopped what I was doing, opened a drawer, pulled out a couple of old carrier bags and took them through to the sitting room where he was kneeling in front of the cold fireplace. "Thanks." He took them from my outstretched hand and turned back to the fire. Glancing back at me, he smiled. "Off you go then – breakfast won't cook itself you know."

I stared at his back as he bent over the grate and, it might have been only for the tiniest micro-second, but everything was suddenly crystal-clear. For that instant, I genuinely wanted to tell him to take his tatty trainers and sweaty clothes and fuck right off but then, just as quickly, the thought of life without him stopped me.

I returned to the kitchen. A full English for brunch was one of my favourite meals, both cooking and eating. The only problem was that I found it impossible not to make a mess and it was while I was clearing up that Richard suggested we go out to a nearby town for a mooch. I smiled delightedly; it was just the sort of thing I enjoyed.

An hour later we were driving through country lanes to the chocolate-box-perfect Cotswold village of Broadway where we spent a very pleasant hour or so strolling up and down the high street, window shopping and dropping into a couple of galleries. Richard found a book on Cotswold walks. "Perhaps there'll be a couple of short ones you'll join me on," he teased, knowing full well that trudging through muddy fields really wasn't my thing; I was more than happy strolling through city streets but had never been that much of a country girl. We were making our way back towards a tea shop when I spotted a pale lilac-with-a-tinge-of-grey dress topped by a matching short-sleeved bolero jacket displayed in the centre of a smart dress shop window. I paused and gazed up at it. It was nice, perhaps a stronger colour would have made it more eye-catching, but nice.

"Just a moment." Richard disappeared into the shop, reappearing seconds later holding a large bag which he held out to me with a rather self-conscious smirk. "You deserve a treat."

I peered inside – there was the dress I'd been looking at seconds earlier. I hugged him. "Oh, my darling – thank you so much." What did I care that it wasn't what I'd have particularly chosen?

He grinned at me. "I like making you smile." For those few precious moments, I really couldn't have been happier.

It was dark by the time we found a café and ordered tea and cakes.

"This is very nice." Richard was leafing through his new book.

"It is," I agreed through a mouthful of very scrumptious lemon gateau.

He laughed. "You really are a hopeless case, aren't you? You just can't resist all this." He gestured towards the contents of the table. "You'll never stick to a diet." I swallowed and stuck my tongue out at which he shook his head and laughed – at me, with me – I really couldn't tell but felt relieved he'd left it at that.

We drove home in companionable silence. Once back, I went upstairs to freshen up; much to my surprise he followed me. I felt his arm round my shoulders. He kissed me gently while his other hand stroked my breast lightly.

I leaned into him. I desperately wanted to hold and be held. I wanted to touch and be touched. I wanted to caress and be caressed. I wanted to tease and be teased. I wanted to want and be wanted. I wanted to fuck and be fucked.

I kissed him, running my hand down his chest to his belt and flicked the buckle open. He pulled away from me slightly. "Wait..." he whispered as he shrugged off his jacket. I stood opposite him, pulled the pink sweater over my head and dropped it on the floor. He mirrored my movements and tugged his black sweatshirt off. We continued to strip until we stood looking at each other in our underwear, He preferred me to be partially clothed so I'd left my bra and knickers on. He shrugged off his underpants and slid into bed. I walked round to his side as unselfconsciously as I could and ran my hands down my body, from shoulders to belly and back again. Even though he was under the duvet, I could see that he was slowly wanking. I leaned over, kissed him, then strutted back to my side of the bed. As I slipped under the cover, very gently I scratched down his chest, following my fingers with my mouth and as I did so, heard him sigh.

I reached down to cover his hand with mine and together we caressed him. I leaned over and started to kiss my way down his body – as I did so he gently but firmly pushed me away. I found myself on my back as Richard set up a firm, insistent rhythm. I clung to him; this time it felt wonderful to be so connected.

One weekday evening, I met Carrie for an after-work drink, naturally at our preferred place.

"Good weekend?" we asked each other as we made ourselves comfortable.

Carrie smirked. I knew what that smirk meant; she'd had a very good weekend.

My smirk was less obvious but there nonetheless. "Yes, it was really nice…" and I went on to tell her how we'd gone out and he'd surprised me with that very unexpected gift. In my eagerness to paint him in a good light I'd completely forgotten about his snippy comments about my weight.

"So, things are going well with you and him?" I was taken aback by a tangible note of concern in her voice, especially after I'd been so enthusiastic.

"Well…" Carrie paused, then took a deep breath. "I really wasn't sure what to do but…" She stared at me intently for a couple of seconds before fumbling in her capacious handbag to pull out her mobile. She tapped for a few moments, then passed it over to me. "Just scroll to the left. Then tell me what you think." She sat back and watched as I looked at a collection of photos, clearly tagged from someone's profile – it showed a biggish party, there must have been at least thirty people. It was in somebody's garden, a large, well-tended garden with a bouncy castle at the end where several children were clearly having the time of their lives. Other photos showed a barbeque with lots of adults standing around with drinks in their hands. It was a sunny day; women were in pretty dresses, some men in shorts and tee-shirts. Nothing at all unusual in that – except that Richard could be clearly seen in some of them and, much more than that, he had his arm round a skinny blonde woman with excessively large tits in a bright pink, low-cut dress; much too low for boobs that big. I spread my fingers on the picture to enlarge it and recognised the woman as Kathleen, someone I'd seen in a photograph he'd shown me some time ago. I felt my chest tighten as I stared, gripping the mobile so hard my knuckles turned white.

Kathleen and her husband, Gary, had known Richard for many years and, about a year ago, poor Gary had unexpectedly dropped dead from a massive heart attack. Very naturally, Kathleen had been shocked and traumatised by this and, to my increasing alarmed surprise, Richard had offered his unstinting support. As time went on my concerns seemed to me to be justified, as this support had transformed itself into seeing her pretty much every week which made me uneasy, anxious and annoyed. Whenever I'd raised the subject, Richard had snapped at me angrily, saying they were just good friends and I was being irrational, silly and downright selfish to have any doubts about his trustworthiness, all of which had only served to fuel my misgivings even more because I'd never been allowed to meet her, despite dropping several very heavy hints that I wanted… no needed… to have the opportunity of confronting her face to face.

I handed the phone back to Carrie. It suddenly hit me just how much Richard was firmly entwined in my life while I'd absolutely been kept on the periphery of his. I felt duped and very stupid and then, to my shocked surprise, tasted the saltiness of hot tears trickling down my cheeks.

"I'm so sorry Lucie. The last thing I wanted to do is hurt you but honestly, I thought you needed to see these." Carrie leaned forward to hold my hand. "But you do know what the trouble is, don't you?" I looked at her. "You've told him how you feel haven't you?" I nodded wordlessly. "But probably in a Lucie-kind-of-way. You know?" I knew exactly what she meant. "Well, don't you think you've kind of enabled this? I mean, you might have been a bit cross and fluffy a couple of times but there's been no real consequences for him. He just shrugs, says you're being silly and you let him get away with it. If him seeing this Kath woman isn't okay, and I certainly wouldn't tolerate it, tell him and mean what you say – don't skirt round the issue otherwise he'll never take you seriously."

"But you know Jake sometimes sees other people," I protested.

"So what? Firstly, he tells me, so I have a choice about whether I go on seeing him or not and anyway, he's still asking why I don't want to live with him so it's kind of fair game that he looks around. I'm really fond of him but it's not the stuff of fairy tales whereas you and Richard – well, that's different. I'm pretty sure he doesn't tell you everything and after five years... it IS five years, isn't it?" I nodded. "You'd expect much more honesty, wouldn't you? And anyway, you want the relationship to move on so it's a whole different ball game. And from what you say, he keeps blocking you from talking about it… frankly that's not the stuff of a committed relationship, not in my book…"

Of course, she was quite right. I'd always had an innate dislike of confrontation which had been my downfall many times. It'd affected a couple of past working relationships and probably made Susie feistier than perhaps she might otherwise have been. I called it being nice and polite; others like Carrie called it being a far-too-easy-going-wuss.

I looked through the pictures again and dug deep to fathom out just what I was feeling. Was it hurt pride? Or was it that I truly loved him and the thought of his betrayal was too much to bear? Or, if I was being brutally honest, was it fear? Fear that at my age he was as good as I was ever going to get. Fear that no-one else would want me because I was fat and didn't have that much money. Fear that I might be on my own for the rest of my life.

Those disquieting thoughts stayed with me off and on until the weekend by which time I'd resolved to tackle him. The truth was I liked… loved him. Even though our 'modus operandi' wasn't ideal I was now so very much used to having him in my life and the thought of being on my own, perhaps wanting, having, to start over again was scarier than I wanted to admit.

On the Friday evening Richard arrived in time for dinner after which we watched a movie and then went to bed where yet again sex felt much too perfunctory for me. But we had a really lovely, relaxed late lunch at one of outside tables at the Boathouse on Saturday. Later found us sitting in my garden in the cool of the early evening with the cats companionably stretched out at our feet. Richard looked completely relaxed and at peace whilst I was feeling anything but.

I lost count of the number of times I opened my mouth to say something, then closed it as visualising what was bound to be a tricky conversation made me feel heart-pumpingly anxious. I was getting quite cross with myself when he made a suggestion.

"I notice Madame Butterfly's on at the Everyman next week." The Everyman was Stratford's local cinema. "Do you fancy going? Friday's the last night. What do you think?"

"How wonderful. Butterfly's my absolute fave. Can't wait." I smiled fondly, all thoughts of starting what was I feared would be a difficult conversation vanished in the face of his unusual thoughtfulness.

Later in bed, it was clear sleep wasn't on his mind. He lay back, arms crossed over his head and grinned at me. "Ok Lucie, over to you." Propping myself up on my elbow, I leaned over to kiss him gently on the forehead, his now-closed eyes, his cheeks and then his mouth. I moved down to his chin, very tenderly scraped my teeth along his jaw, feeling rather than hearing his soft sigh. I nibbled down his throat onto his chest, gently bit his nipples and then let my tongue trace downwards towards his belly button. I was thinking to give a blow job but felt his hands pull me up, so straddled him instead and, as I slowly lowered myself onto him, stared deep into his eyes. He gripped my hips so tightly it hurt, but I barely felt any pain as we set a rhythm that got faster and faster until he bucked, groaned, then slumped back with his eyes closed. He was almost asleep by the time I'd rolled off him.

As ever, we talked on the phone a couple of times during the week.

"I'm feeling like a holiday…" My heart lifted as I thought of a few days away. "I quite fancy going to Cuba for a few weeks, is that something you could afford?"

My heart sank as quickly as it had risen. He knew full well that taking 'a few weeks' out of my diary, certainly at the moment, would be very difficult – not to mention the cost. "Well, Richard, I'd have to think about it. But if I can't manage Cuba, perhaps we could take a little break closer to home?" The words sounded small and petty as I said them; I was pretty sure what his reaction would be and I was right.

"I want decent holidays before I'm too old to properly enjoy them. I really don't see why I have to wait until you manage your affairs better. Really Lucie, this scraping around for money is ridiculous at your age…"

The argument continued for several minutes with both of us sticking to our entrenched standpoints until he finally said, "You know, I think I'm just going to go anyway. If you can't come then I'll find someone who can…" and it was on this note that we put our phones down.

However, the following evening when we talked, it was as if that conversation had never taken place – neither of us mentioned it and afterwards when I thought a bit more about it, it seemed it had all been forgotten – just a storm in a teacup I decided with a sigh of relief.

By seven the following Friday, we were happily settled on a cosy sofa at the Everyman, munching sweet-and-salty popcorn – my favourite cinema snack. The production was, as expected, breathtakingly enjoyable; as always, Butterfly's final haunting aria when she kills herself moments before Pinkerton arrives, calling her name, moved me to tears. Much as I preferred 'proper' live theatre, it had to be admitted this was almost as good.

We were strolling home when, after saying what a lovely evening it'd been, I suggested that the next time perhaps we could see a real live opera, maybe in London?

"That's a really good idea Lucie. Actually, I saw the Marriage of Figaro in town recently. It was excellent. You know, I think I've been bitten by the opera bug."

Within a few steps, my happiness had seeped away. I was pretty sure he wouldn't have gone to the opera on his own – so who'd been with him? Infuriatingly, the answer was all too obvious. "You went with Kath – didn't you?" He was silent. "You went with her; I know you did. You just don't care how I feel about her, do you? Just why the fuck do you think this is okay?"

"For Christ's sake, stop banging on about it." He looked, and sounded, furious. "You know what? You've just ruined a wonderful evening."

"Oh no, don't you dare blame this on me. It wouldn't be quite so bad, perhaps, if you'd told me or even if I'd met her but you keep behaving like it's a dirty little secret." A sudden thought struck me. "You like all this don't you? Having a weekday woman as well as a weekend woman? You love it…" I grabbed his arm and stared up at him where I saw shifty anger in his pale blue eyes.

"Oh, for fuck's sake, just leave me alone, will you?" He was positively growling as he wrenched his arm from me, turned away and, hands in pockets, head bowed, strode off home ahead of me.

As I slowly followed, an old memory flooded back to me; I'd been tackling a particularly tricky crossword one weekend when Richard looked across at me: "What are you doing Lucie?"

"Thought I'd have a go at this. Want to lend a hand?"

"Sure. I like crosswords.'" He'd smiled reflectively: "I do the Telegraph one most days."

"Really? I didn't realise you were that much of a crossword devotee."

"Mmmm. I do it over the phone with Kathy. She really enjoys…" His voice had faded away as he'd looked at my disbelieving face. "Well, you know I talk with her and she misses doing the crossword with Gary, so we do it together over the phone. She suggested it ages ago and I was only too happy to oblige." He looked at me, almost angrily. "Now, don't start, Lucie. We've had a lovely day so don't spoil it."

I knew what I wanted to say but his last few words had robbed me of the power of speech so I sat in silence, struggling to make sense of his oh-so-casual revelation. I'd felt shocked, angry, frightened and vulnerable all at the same time.

Whenever I'd subsequently reflected, on that conversation, I liked to think that he'd genuinely missed the point as to why I was so upset. The fact that he was on the phone with her nearly every day wasn't something he'd have called intimate. And when he'd told me that it was her who almost invariably called him rather than the other way around, he didn't seem to think that was odd in any way. Once, half-jokingly but in fact had really meant it, I'd called her a 'bunny boiler' all he'd done was laugh before again saying that I was being ridiculous. And when I'd asked him what he'd have felt were the positions to be reversed, that I spent such a long time on the phone with another man almost daily, he had no answer.

This time. his response was to flounce out, saying it was me who didn't understand and that I should be 'nicer'. After throwing his few things into his holdall, he'd stood in the doorway, case in hand, looking down at me. "So, do you want me to go?"

"You know perfectly well what I want." I'd stared up at him, unsure whether to laugh or cry at the absurdity of his take on the situation. "I want you never to see that awful woman again. I want you never ever to talk to her again. I want us to be happy together but we can't while she's around and you continue to dignify her disgraceful behaviour." He'd taken a breath to say something but I'd stopped him. "Honestly, I don't know how you can treat me so badly Richard.

Shut the door behind you please." My mother had always impressed on me the need for good manners.

So, as often was the case after an argument, he'd left and we'd not spoken for a few days before, albeit waveringly, we'd managed to get back on some sort of track. He continued to declare that doing the crossword with her was simply the mark of friendship and he had no romantic interest in her whatsoever. And, because I'd so wanted to believe him, I'd had to come to be more or less content with that.

I'd half-expected him to be in his car by the time I got home but no, there he was, sitting on the small bench by the front door looking, I had to say, a bit contrite. I opened the door and, almost reluctantly, let him in.

We slept back-to-back, not touching, that night.

Early the next morning, he reached across and held me gently. He kissed my face, my neck, my shoulders, my breasts. Even though the memory of what happened last night was firmly in my head, I returned his kisses and reached down for him but my hand was gently pushed away. He held my hands above my head and softly bit my neck and shoulders before abruptly starting to fuck me. His urgency fuelled my desire but he came quickly which left me yet again twitching with frustration. He lay back and closed his eyes. "You carry on without me." I didn't.

I stood under the shower and let the scalding hot water cascade over me and then, completely out of the blue, remembered a line from one of my all-time favourite movies, Tootsie, when Sandy says '1 read the Second Sex... and the Cinderella Complex! I'm responsible for my own orgasms...' and thought, well yes, I might well be responsible for mine but surely my partner could, at the very least, stay awake for the event? As I rubbed myself dry, I nodded to myself – the time was coming for me to speak up, I simply had to.

Rather oddly, to my mind, he made it a point of trying to stay friends with his exes, something he'd told me a long time ago and which I'd never understood. 'Surely an ex is an ex for a reason' I'd said and he'd simply smiled inscrutably and told me I didn't understand. I'd accepted his history, what else could I do? But when, some time ago now, he'd told me he'd met one of them for lunch, it'd made me uneasy.

And last year, when I was being 'silly and irrational' as he'd infuriatingly put it, he did let slip that Kath had had a bit of a 'thing' for him way back when he was married and I'd fleetingly wondered just how far that 'thing' had gone.

So, of course the subject of Kath raised its ugly head yet again a bit later when I was feeling brave. And yet again he said he'd known her for a very long time, they were just friends, and because she was in a 'dark place' the least he could do was be supportive. All he'd done was go with her to a family get-together where he knew a few people. And yet-a-bloody-gain, he'd managed to make me feel confused and guilty.

I felt so torn. On the one hand I wanted to get rid of all the uncertainty and upset, but on the other hand I cared deeply about him, and knew he did me. So, despite all the talking, we reached no conclusion.

Luckily, I was incredibly busy in the week which was a huge distraction from the emotional turmoil of the weekend. Once I'd found, I suppose it felt like my true calling, I'd thoroughly enjoyed teaching and all that went with it. I'd been lucky enough to work in colleges and universities and whilst the politics in education had driven me scatty, I adored the contact with bright young minds. Now that I was semi-retired and freelance, I loved my work-life balance. For so long I'd been more than happy to be defined by my work, taking great pride in it, and was delighted to have been able to keep and even attract clients successfully beyond the official age of retirement.

It was lunchtime on a day when I was delivering a workshop on time management. As usual, I was sitting with a few of my trainees. Two of the men were talking and I found myself listening, at first absent-mindedly and then more attentively. "It's just not right," one of them said; the other nodded in agreement. Apparently, his partner was seeing another man, someone she'd known for years. "But I'm sure there's more in it than meets the eye…" The other man nodded again. "Just because they're friends from way back doesn't make it okay. She's seeing him more and more often; the kids have told me she's often late home, too late to make their tea on time. And anyway, if she wants to go out, it ought to be with me." More nods.

They didn't reach any real conclusion about what he should do but did agree that having an active social life with someone else really wasn't tolerable. And as I listened, I thought of Richard.

I thought about that conversation a lot over the next few days and by the time Richard arrived that weekend, I'd come to a decision.

As so often is the case, that decision was put on hold when he walked in; he was very upbeat and affectionate. We ordered a delicious Indian takeaway; I'd been tempted by Kashmiri Chicken, not realising quite so hot it would be – along with the spiciness that made my nose run and left my lips swollen and burning, there was an unexpected tinge of sweetness that was wonderful. Afterwards, we sat together in front of the TV as we half-watched an old movie, it was shades of our earlier days when it'd felt we were truly in synch with each other.

The film drew to a close. "Bed – now," he said in a tone that I knew brooked no argument.

Upstairs he hugged me tightly; despite the many let-downs both emotional and erotic, there had always been a physical attraction between us and the pull was very strong.

His kisses were more tender and passionate than they'd been for a long time. I ran my fingertips over his shoulders, down his arms and onto his hands which I guided across my body. I pushed his hands down my torso to my hips as I gently nibbled on his neck and shoulders. He ran his hands down my back and bottom to my thighs, gently pinching as he did so, pulling me into him. I squirmed against him, desperate to feel as much of his body against me as possible and again reached for his hands, holding them firmly against my breasts, caressing and kneading myself through him, shivering with desire and anticipation. He suddenly pushed me back and before I could draw breath, started fucking me with a force and intensity that made me gasp and whimper.

He came quickly but instead of his usual turning away, held me close and continued caressing me. I luxuriated under his touch and minutes later arched my back. "Don't stop, oh God... please... please... don't stop..." He obediently continued to kiss and nuzzle my shoulders and neck while softly fondling my breasts. I felt surges of pleasure engulf me and as the final paroxysms dwindled, closed my eyes in blissful contentment and snuggled into him.

Action on any decision would wait.

Over breakfast, I raised the subject of my disquiet. And it wasn't just Kath. As gently and empathetically as I could, I talked about our relationship – how wonderful it would be if our lives were more entwined, if we saw more of each other, if things were more inclusive... He sat unusually quietly, nodding occasionally, as if he was agreeing with me.

Then came the bombshells, one after the other.

"Well, well, Lucie. You're saying you want more" I nodded, probably more eagerly than I should have done. "What about you not sticking to a diet? What about the fact that you're actually putting on weight? What about you not being that fit?" I sat with my mouth open. "And apart from this fitness thing that you know bothers me, you never seem to know when the next bit of work comes in – you do all sorts of bits and bobs; why, you've even had foreign students stay in the summer – it's all a bit ad hoc isn't it?" I could have sworn he looked as though he was enjoying himself. "All you do is bleat on about love..." he snorted derisorily, "...it's ludicrous..." He paused for a moment. "And you're still paying a mortgage? Well, at your age that's absurd – frankly it's just not good enough..." He stood; pale blue eyes cold and flinty. "Don't you see I can't possibly make any real commitment until I'm sure we could afford the lifestyle I... we want. I've no intention of diminishing my life by being with you..."

Enough really was enough. "Stop. Just stop right now." I was shaking, mainly with fury. "Can't you hear how awful that sounds? You want a balance sheet and profit and loss account of my circumstances and then you'll decide if I'm a good enough bet or not? Really? So, everything comes down to money, does it? How fucking dare you say stuff like that?" I was on a roll now and absolutely nothing was going to stop me. "How can you possibly think that any of that's okay? And..." Another thought crystalised. "Is that why you're seeing that bloody cow? Keeping her sweet while you decide what to do with me?"

"You really think I'm that petty? Oh Lucie, why do you always have to think the worst of me? Why don't you trust me?"

He wanted me to trust him? "So, how often are you seeing her?"

He suddenly looked shifty. "Well... once... twice a week I suppose..." He saw my look of incredulity. "I didn't tell you because I knew you wouldn't understand..." That old chestnut I thought as I heard yet more puerile excuses being trotted out as he continued trying to justify his actions.

I interrupted him. "You know, it's one thing to bumble on as we are but it's quite another for you to see another woman. Sleep with her probably…" It was a throwaway remark but I saw guilt written all over his face.

"If you don't trust me, then what future do we have?" His voice was plaintive. What the fuck I thought, as what I'd decided days ago crashed back into my mind.

"Maybe… maybe we don't…" It felt like those three little words were being dragged out of me – even at that point when I'd felt pushed to my absolute limit, I wasn't absolutely sure they were what I wanted to say.

"What?" His voice was tinged with anger and disbelief.

Now I meant them. "Like you said; maybe we're done. I've had enough of all your criticisms, your unkindness, you still seeing Kath. You know full well how much you seeing her bothers and hurts me but it doesn't seem to register with you, not one bit. I kind of understood you seeing her after Gary died – that she needed consolation – but that's a long time ago. She must have other friends she can lean on. Ad why do you allow her to dictate whether I can meet her or not? It looks like you care more about her than you do about me and that's not ok, not right, when it's me you're meant to be in a relationship with, not her."

"I…"

"No, don't interrupt." I took a deep breath. "You're actually treating us both unfairly – her because it's blatantly obvious she wants to be more than just friends with you, and me because it's totally unreasonable, not to mention hugely disrespectful, to spend so much time with someone who's got that kind of agenda. Unless you're sleeping with her that is, which would be disgusting." I wrinkled my nose at the thought – God, you'd want to dip it in bleach for a bloody long time before letting it get near you, I thought and involuntarily smiled at the mental picture. "You do realise you shagging her would break my trust completely, not to mention how despicable it'd be of her to treat another woman so appallingly." I imagined my two trainees applauding my bravado and half-smiled at the thought.

"Lucie, I promise you, I'm not sleeping with her."

I stared at him – that's all you can say, I thought. Really? Sidestepping as usual. "That doesn't make any difference. Cheating isn't just about sex – it's about a betrayal of trust. Or don't you get that?" I stared at him intently, but couldn't fathom what he was thinking – or feeling. "I think we both need some time. Time to think. You need to consider if you can put up with all of my 'issues'. What I certainly don't need is being constantly put down – I deserve support, not continual criticism. You need to make up your mind whether you're going to continue 'consoling' her and lose me, or stop seeing her and try to save what we have."

I wasn't able to finish with him completely – not quite yet.

"Are you giving me an ultimatum?" Clearly, he was amazed.

"I'm saying I think we need a break and when... if... we come back from that break, I expect her to be out of our lives."

He sat in silence. I could almost see the cogs turning in his head.

"Maybe you're right." I'd half-expected, hoped, he'd protest his love for me – but no. "We both need to think about some things."

He walked past me, went upstairs to collect his stuff and returned to the hallway.

"Well then... I don't know when I'll see you..." His hand reached for the front door, he opened it slowly and stepped out. It was almost as though he expected me to pull him back.

I had to say something. "You know I love you. But we need some time to think things through."

I watched from the doorway as he got into the car and drove away. I stood until I couldn't hear his car any longer. Once inside, I began to cry as I realised what had happened. What was I going to do now? Would we ever get back together? Had I lost my last chance of love? My sobbing turned to frustrated wailing – seemed my decision had come at an awfully high price.

By the evening and after chats with a couple of girlfriends, I was feeling much better. And as time passed, I knew I'd been right all along. We had to take time away from each other so we could properly examine our lives carefully and, hopefully, return to each other refreshed – positively in love with each other, determined to be together – and no one else. I reassured myself that loads of people in tricky relationships took breaks and came back to each other stronger and more in love than ever before.

The next few days were amazingly peaceful…

Chapter 2

C arrie and I had agreed to meet at the Dirty
Duck at six before going on to the theatre;
we'd managed to get a couple of the much cheaper
residents' tickets that morning. Even though she'd
told me she was exhausted, she still managed to
look her usual glamorous self in a short navy shift
dress with thick matching tights and flat loafers. She
gulped down half of her large gin and tonic before
describing her dreadful week. Apparently, her boss
had been particularly difficult. "It's got to the point
where I don't feel there's any option other than look
for something else." We talked about it at length.
"Anyway, Lucie. Are you okay?" I was, I really was,
and she silently clapped her approval.

Feminists though we aspired to be, we thoroughly
enjoyed a typically magnificent production of The
Taming Of The Shrew; one of the undoubted benefits
of living in Stratford was that so often we were able
to enjoy the most amazing live theatre.

Afterwards, we bought some chips and ate them
as we strolled back to her's where I'd left my car. "I'm
so pleased you're coping okay," Carrie said.

"Well, not all the time," I admitted. She shot me a suspicious look so I told her what Val, a mutual friend, had said.

I didn't see Val that often, she wasn't a particularly close friend, but our kids had been in the same class at primary school and we'd occasionally chatted as we waited for them at the end of their day. Like me, she was on the large side but, unlike me, had a rather stern look about her, always wearing what I called 'sensible' shoes; it wasn't that I didn't wear comfortable flats myself but her lace-up brogues seemed overly so. I'd bumped into her a few days previously and we'd spent an hour or so together. Val was married; her now-husband had been married to someone else when they met and, after a lengthy affair with her, he'd left his wife. It had been on Val's insistence they married; I knew from local gossip he hadn't been that keen at the time but they seemed to rub along reasonably well – it was common knowledge she kept him on a pretty tight leash. When I'd told Val that Richard and I were on a break, she'd urged me not to let it go on for too long. "He'll stray, they all do. Best that you know what he's doing even if it's what you don't like, at least you can keep tabs on him. And anyway, it's so much nicer to have a man in your life. Being single isn't that great, you know…" There was lots more in the same vein so by the time we said our goodbyes, I'd felt dejected, fleetingly questioning the wisdom of what I'd done.

"And what does everyone else say?"

I stopped to think for a few seconds. "Actually, everyone else I've talked to has said I've done exactly the right thing and most say I shouldn't take him back even if he wants to. You know – leopards and spots?"

Carrie nodded. She knew exactly what I meant. Her ex-husband, an extremely good looking and, on the surface, charming man, had been a serial philander until eventually after many years she'd had enough and, much to his amazement, had kicked him into touch.

In some of our franker discussions, Richard had admitted he'd behaved in much the same way in the past but now that he was older and wiser, he realised the foolishness of his actions. At the time, I'd believed him – but now? Possibly… probably not.

One morning when as usual, rather blearily I checked my phone for any messages, to my astonishment, there was one from Richard. My heart raced. I hovered one finger tentatively over the message before forcing myself to open it. 'Lucie. We need to talk. I'll come up this weekend. Rx'

Not a question I noted, just an assumption I'd be ready and waiting for him. I lay back to consider my reply. 'Yes, we do indeed. I'm busy in the morning so what about 3ish on Saturday? L x'. I wasn't busy but certainly wasn't going to let him know that.

When I heard a knock at the door, I took a deep breath before opening it. "Hello Richard." He didn't quite look himself, not scruffy exactly but just that little bit less sharp that usual and when I stood aside to let him in, wasn't met with the usual waft of Oud Wood cologne hitting my nose – indeed I could have sworn there was just the merest hint of old sweat, as if the shirt he was wearing wasn't freshly washed.

There was an awkward silence. "Tea or coffee?" I deliberately kept away from booze in case he – or I – decided that he should go sooner than later. He was settled at his usual place on the sofa and smiled his thanks as I handed him his favourite mug.

"So..."

"So..." I echoed.

"Where to start... I've been thinking a lot. You know, I've missed you so much more than I ever thought I would." He took a deep breath. "Look, I do appreciate you're making efforts to get a bit fitter and that, along with your already better eating habits, can only improve your health. I only keep on about these things because I want you to be healthier so you're around for as long as possible and we have as much time together as we can. And as far as your money and work situation is concerned? Well, we do have to talk more about that because it does concern me, certainly if we end up living together, but... I do understand things are tricky in your line of work and you don't want a full-time job at your age. I'm sure you're doing the best you can."

For the entire duration of his little speech my eyes were wide and my jaw had dropped open – although he'd said he'd missed me, there was so much more negative than positive. I drew breath as the thought that I'd not given him a drink-drink so could tell him to fuck off flashed into my mind. I really wasn't prepared for what came next though.

"But despite all this, I love you… and I want you. I want 'us' to work, I really do."

All negativity tumbled out of my head. "I love you too, Richard."

He'd got to his feet and leaned over me. We held each other in a long embrace – I could have stayed like that forever. "I've missed you so much," I whispered.

He moved his hands to clasp my arms, pulling me to my feet. He kissed me deeply and motioned us towards the door, guiding me up the stairs. I couldn't resist, desperately wanting to feel a close connection.

Upstairs, he did a real unexpected – he slowly undressed me, kissing my exposed skin as each piece of clothing was removed. It was teasingly divine. He pulled off his own clothes in-between kisses. I reached down to his hardness, moving my hand firmly. He groaned, then pushed me backwards to sit, then lie back on the bed. Climbing on top of me, we kissed passionately before he moved down to my breasts, while his hands caressed me just the way he knew I liked. I was writhing underneath him. He knelt between my legs and I gasped as we locked together – our passion and excitement overwhelming us. He set a steady, insistent rhythm. I tried to match him, both of us gasping for air as the intensity and speed inexorably rose. His body arched and I was overcome with wave after wave of warm tingling spasms flooding through me. I clung to him wanting that wonderful closeness to last forever.

We stayed like that for a couple of minutes in silence before disentangling ourselves.

"That was..."

"Yes, it was, wasn't it?"

We lay, blissfully entwined, my head resting on his shoulder, and drifted into drowsiness.

It was dark when we opened our eyes. We were still tangled together but hunger drove us out of bed. Not bothering to get dressed, I pulled on my pink satin dressing gown and padded downstairs to make a start on dinner. As I prepared a salad of warm chicken and couscous spiked with shredded vegetables, olive oil and balsamic vinegar, I smiled at the memory of the passion and closeness we'd shared. Afterwards, and unusually, he cleared the plates, telling me to sit and rest as I'd done the cooking. Wow, I thought, he certainly has been doing some thinking and, perhaps cynically, I wondered how long it would last.

Later in bed, we fell asleep with his arm around my shoulders and mine draped over his torso. Perfect, I thought, just perfect.

We were in exactly the same position when I woke up to find Richard awake and gazing at me – how beguiling was that? Later, as I served brunch, he looked up at me. "Thank you, Lucie. You do treat me well, don't you?" I smiled coyly. We returned to bed enjoying each other for another couple of hours. We talked. We laughed. We made love. It all felt so natural and right.

It was during one of our mid-week chats when Richard said he'd booked a couple of tickets to see Two Gentlemen of Verona at Warwick Arts Centre. "It'll be in..." There was a pause and I heard a couple of pages being riffled through, "…three weeks. That okay?"

"That sounds really lovely darling. What a wonderful surprise."

The following Saturday was fine and dry so we decided to take the train to nearby Birmingham for a change. The next few hours passed very pleasantly meandering round the shops before buying a couple of sandwiches to eat in the gardens surrounding St Phillip's Cathedral. Crocuses had pushed their way through the shaggy grass and the bright yellows, whites and purples made the square look jauntily welcoming.

"Right Lucie, I have to talk to you about Kathy…" Oh Jesus, not again I thought as I sighed impatiently. "No, no – wait – please hear me out." He took a deep breath. "I've told her very clearly that she and I are friends…" I opened my mouth. "Platonic friends," he added quickly. I closed my mouth. "But Lucie, there's history between us and I simply can't cut her out of my life completely. So…" He fumbled in his pocket. "This is to reassure you…" He held out a small square box.

Mystified, I opened it to see a ring – a thin gold band of tiny sapphires and diamonds. I blinked in disbelief.

"It's not an engagement ring," he said hastily. "It's a… a commitment ring. To show you how I feel."

Eagerly I tried it on but, to my disappointment, it only just fit my left pinkie.

He looked down at my hand. "Hmmm… thought your fingers were thinner. Oh well, never mind. Looks good though. Does the job, doesn't it?" He was looking awfully pleased with himself.

Of course, I thanked him profusely – what else could I do? So why, I wondered on the journey home gazing down at my left hand, did it feel strange, not quite right. Mentally I shook my head impatiently at myself; this was a much bigger step than I'd ever imagined he'd make and wasn't it exactly what I'd been wanting for so long?

That evening we were due to meet two friends of mine, Shona and James who'd I'd known for well over forty years. They looked like the perfect couple. Both were tall and slim and both dressed in classically unstated clothes. I'd long given up aspiring to emulate Shona's style but had always admired it. James had taken early retirement several years previously and Shona, an outstanding primary school teacher, had followed him shortly afterwards. They spent at least half the year travelling so always had stories that I found fascinating when we met, which I tried to do at least once a month when they were back home.

We'd arranged to meet at Loxleys, a lovely bistro in the heart of the town.

"If James is as dull as he was last time, I swear I'll drown myself in the bloody finger bowl." He knew I was going to order mussels.

I couldn't believe what he'd just said. "You behave or I'll drown YOU in the finger bowl." I thought that little joke would be the end of it.

"I don't know why they've asked us. She obviously hates me, and he bores the arse off me." Richard found their ongoing travelogues a tad tedious.

I was wrong, that wasn't the end of it. "Now Richard. Please. I've been looking forward to this evening for ages. Just be nice – it's only for a couple of hours." I didn't like to add that they were amongst the very few of my friends who'd welcomed us into their social life.

The whole thing was an unmitigated disaster. Richard was teasingly provocative from the outset which irritated me, and the others, beyond belief. When I showed Shona my 'commitment' ring I was met with slightly amused disbelief. "Couldn't he at least have got something that fitted you?" Clearly, she was unimpressed. Halfway through our cheeseboard, Richard and Shona had a pointless argument that rumbled on for what seemed like forever. And I had to admit that James wasn't his sparkling best, so by the time we parted, Richard was pricklier than ever.

"God, they're awful people," Richard said as we walked away.

"How bloody dare you be so rude to my friends…" Normally I'd have agreed, or pretended to agree with him but this time I was genuinely livid.

"She's argumentative and he's boring. They're not interested in me at all."

"Really? Well, frankly I don't care if you like them or not, they're my oldest and dearest friends. I asked you to be nice and you weren't, the very opposite in fact. Is that the respect you give me, or my friends? Not okay Richard. Honestly, enough really is enough…"

The argument continued. I think it was when I said, "I ask you to be agreeable and all you can do is act like a sulky teenager," that was the trigger for another belligerent outburst from him.

We walked the rest of the way home in silence and in bed lay back-to-back, making sure we didn't touch. So much for 'I love you' and 'commitment' I thought as uneasy sleep eventually swept over me.

I was still feeling peeved in the morning but, almost automatically, started cooking breakfast. Minutes later, he appeared at the door. "Oh, so you're cooking us brunch, are you?" Not a smidge of an apology.

Instantly my anger was rekindled. "Well, I'm not fucking playing tennis, am I?" I silently tutted at myself – was that the best I could muster?

Silently, he slunk off to set the table. I decided not to comment about his forgetting the napkins as usual, and served up in silence.

He looked down at his plate, then across at me. "My egg's broken." He sounded just like a small child. I desperately wanted to laugh but managed to keep a straight face. Picking up the bottle of brown sauce, he shook it a bit too vigorously, so much so that sauce splodged out in one huge splat. I kept my eyes firmly on my plate trying to stop my shoulders shaking with inner giggles – it was all too clear he hadn't seen the funny side of it.

We finished brunch and, again unusually, he cleared the table. "Coffee?" I nodded.

He made the coffee. "Look Lucie, I never meant to embarrass you. I'm not that keen on them but they're your friends and I had no right to make things difficult for you."

Never one to bear a long-term grudge, I hugged my forgiveness.

One weekday evening I thought to call Richard instead of my normal waiting for him to ring but there was no answer. I tried again half an hour later – again no answer. Shortly afterwards a text came through. 'Have had a very busy day. Just had dinner as thanks. Been enjoying wine so will drink coffee for a while. Should be heading home in about an hour. All is well!! Rxxx'. All was well? When I knew he was almost certainly with Kath? As far as I was concerned all was bloody well not well. I didn't return his text – I saw no point in doing so.

After a restless night, I was woken by my phone ringing.

"Good morning Lucie. Sorry I didn't call last night but it was too late by the time I got home." He sounded as if he didn't have a care in the world. I asked what had made him so late. "Oh, I was at Kathy's." So, my suspicions had been right. "You know she's recently moved into a flat? I'm sure I mentioned it. Anyway, I popped over to put up some shelves, build a couple of flat-pack units – that kind of thing." I remained silent. "Well, you know me – I'm quite good at practical stuff and it makes me feel good to help out. Yesterday I worked from early morning to about seven, when she insisted on giving me dinner. She talked a great deal about missing Gary as well as her general worries, much of it said between floods of tears. I hope I said the right things to console her." He'd spoken quickly, as if to block me from saying anything. "So, did you have a good day?"

If he thought to provoke me into an argument, he'd be waiting a long time. "Lovely thank you Richard. Really good…" And I left it at that, suspecting that he wanted to know more but was resisting the temptation to ask. Maybe, just maybe, I thought as we said our goodbyes, ignoring the whole sorry mess was better than this continual confrontation.

I kept to my usual routine of shopping before the weekend to buy foods I knew he really liked along with yet another litre bottle of Southern Comfort. I'd decided on a retro menu for Friday evening of prawn cocktail followed by steak diane and mini sherry trifles.

To my delighted amazement he came bearing a large bunch of red roses, the second time in five years that he'd bought me flowers. "Thank you so much – they're beautiful." As I stood on tiptoe to kiss his cheek, the memory of Alex bringing me flowers every Friday evening flooded my mind; sometimes a single rose, sometimes some hedgerow flowers he seen and thought I'd like and, when we could afford it, what he'd say was a 'proper' bunch of fragrant blooms. It had taken me many years to get used to buying my own flowers. He shrugged, looking a bit self-conscious. "I know how much you girlies like flowers and wanted to make you smile." He grinned at me. "And it has." He looked smugly pleased with himself.

He was profuse in his compliments about the menu I'd produced which I found pleasing and touching in equal measure.

Later, in bed, he turned to me. Taking my left hand, he kissed each finger, then kissed and softly bit my shoulder. His fingertips brushed against my hipbone, I pushed against his hand and ran my nails gently over his chest. Much as I was loving his caresses I couldn't stop shaking with impatience. Seconds later we were locked tightly together. I felt his body tremble as he came. This time I didn't care I hadn't – his appreciation of my culinary efforts, the closeness of the evening – all that was more than enough.

It was with the thought the commitment ring really must have meant something deeply significant and, at long last, things were really working out that I fell asleep.

On the Saturday afternoon I was due to meet some girlfriends; it was a long-standing arrangement and I knew Richard was fine with that. I had a lovely couple of gossipy hours but was more than ready to go home when we hugged our goodbyes. As I opened my front door, I sniffed – the smell of cooking was unmistakable. I went through to find him in the kitchen, wearing one of my aprons, a little frilly one that made me giggle, stirring something in a saucepan with a look of rapt concentration on his face. The meal was nothing particularly elaborate – roast chicken plus a few trimmings – but the fact he'd bothered to do anything at all was remarkable. We sat at the table for ages, listening to music, talking and laughing – it was a wonderful evening.

We cleared away together and then sprawled on the sofa, sipping our second glass of wine.

After a while, I went to refill our refills which I brought in together with some small oatmeal biscuits and cheese. "To soak up the booze," I explained as I handed him a plate.

We nibbled on the cheese and biscuits and polished off the refills. As I reached for Richard's glass, he held my hand. "No more Lucie, otherwise I won't make it up the stairs." We both laughed and snuggled back down on the sofa to watch an old movie that I actually enjoyed. As the credits rolled, he ran his fingertips up and down my arm and nuzzled into my neck. "Bed?" His voice was muffled through my hair.

In bed he continued to nuzzle my neck. "Spoons?" He fumbled for my breasts and rubbed my nipples a little harder than I'd have liked while he kissed the back of my neck and shoulders. I was too squiffy to feel sexy and it was a relief to realise he was way too flaccid to manage much, clearly the wine had taken its toll on him too.

With a muttered "Oh fuck it…" he rolled over onto his back and thankfully I moved to face him, running my hand over his chest, down his stomach to start a gentle rhythm but it was very obvious semi-hard was the best he could manage. However, after a few strokes he came with a small moan and seconds later I heard his breathing deepen.

Two Gentlemen of Verona was wonderfully acted and presented, telling the story of friendship, love, normal Shakespearean cross-dressing, betrayal and eventual reconciliation. "Well, Proteus was a bit of a shit, wasn't he?" Richard sounded amused.

"Absolutely was but, amazingly, Julia forgives him."

"You think she shouldn't have done that?"

"Probably not but then she loves him and people in love tend to forgive, don't they?" I gave him what I hoped was a meaningful look which was probably wasted on him.

Once home, he silently took me by the hand and led me upstairs. After lighting the candles on the dressing table, he kissed my cheek, my neck, my shoulders and then returned to my face which he cupped in his hands before kissing me deeply and tenderly. I responded to his kisses with longing and passion – then scattered butterfly kisses on his forehead, eyes, cheeks, chin and throat before working down to kiss and nibble his chest and nipples while my hand drifted down across his belly, skirted his crotch and caressed his thighs. I heard him sigh and softly moan and then felt him, very gently, pull me back towards his face.

"Hey, no hurry. No hurry at all," he breathed into my mouth as he kissed me and then moved his head down to softly bite my neck. "Time for me to watch you play." I gasped before realising he was gazing at me with a gentle intensity.

I leaned away from him to push an extra pillow under my shoulders so that I was reclining, raised my hands to my throat and putting them back-to-back, ran them between my breasts down to my thighs and back again, this time flat against my skin unable to stop my body pushing against them. Much as I was in the moment and wanted to be as abandoned as possible, I felt hazily self-conscious and closed my eyes as I softly scratched my way back to my breasts and encircled my nipples with my middle fingers, arching my back as I did so.

"Look at me," I shook my head. He put his hand over one of mine, caressed me through my hand and then abruptly stopped. "Look at me Lucie." I obeyed and he smiled down at me. "Good girl. I want to watch you come before I fuck you." I gasped – this was shades of our early days when going to bed was far more captivatingly exciting than our now normal, routinely predictable sex. I managed to continue gazing into Richard's eyes as I licked my fingers before gliding my hands down my body to my inner thighs to start a slow, deliberate pressure and rhythm that rapidly became faster and faster as ripples of sensuality and desire overtook me. I tried to slow down but couldn't and as I closed my eyes, arching backwards, was hit by spasms of pleasure. I lightened my touch and squirmed my way to more and still more shudders of delight.

As my breathing started to return to normal, I opened my eyes to see Richard staring at me, holding his tumescent cock. He almost growled as he fucked me hard and fast – I was still in a post-orgasmic haze of tingling sensitivity, but his excitement was infectious and as he reached his explosive climax, I revelled in a another, altogether gentler, orgasm. He collapsed over me for a few seconds and then rolled off, still panting.

"Wow," I said softly.

"Wow indeed."

And moments later we were asleep in each other's arms.

I was awake earlier than normal for a weekend. Richard was fast asleep next to me and I dropped a light kiss on his cheek before getting out of bed as quietly as I could. As I stood under the hot shower, the memories of last night replayed in my head and I smiled. This weekend, more than ever before, had convinced me that all was well with us and I closed my eyes in sheer delight at the thought of our future together. After pulling on black leggings and a baggy pale grey sweater before applying a little makeup, I went into the kitchen to make some tea which I took upstairs. Richard was still asleep so I left his mug and tip-toed back downstairs. I heard his footsteps about ten minutes later as he made his way to the bathroom.

He joined me a few minutes later. He looked a bit uptight which I didn't understand. I stood with a smile. "Fresh cup, darling?"

He handed me his empty mug. "Please, that would be nice."

As I made fresh tea, he wandered into the garden and spent a few minutes gathering up some fallen twigs and leaves. How sweet I thought, how kind.

When he came back in, he looked stressed. "Lucie…" For some reason, I suddenly felt sick but couldn't tell whether it was in fear or pleasurable excitement – was this the time he was going to propose a real commitment? He stopped and cleared his throat. "I… I just can't do this."

I could have sworn my heart actually stopped. "What? What are you talking about?"

He looked down at his clasped hands. "This just isn't good enough, I…" He was almost whispering.

"What? What's not good enough? What are you talking about Richard?"

"Us… This…" he swept his arm vaguely. "It's not enough. Not for me. Enough really is enough."

Now my heart was pounding so hard I was sure he must have been able to hear it – I could.

As I closed my eyes in shocked pain, I felt him walk past me to the door and heard his footsteps going upstairs. Against my will but unable to stop, I followed him into the spare room to see him packing. He looked up. "It's no good any more. You do know that, don't you?"

Of course, I didn't know that. I'd believed him when he'd kissed me. I'd believed him when we'd made love the previous evening. I'd believed him when he'd said he loved me. I'd believed him when he'd assured me that bloody Kath and he were really just platonic friends so I had nothing to worry about. I'd believed him when he'd given me the 'commitment' ring. And certainly, after the last two such wonderfully loving days it seemed inconceivable, ludicrously so, that we were over. The full realisation of what he was saying cut through me like a knife and I bent over slightly as yet more shocked pain ripped through my body. I couldn't believe the timing of this abrupt ending... at this calculated cruelty.

"But... but..." I was lost for words. "Didn't the last couple of days mean anything to you? Was it all just a game?" He looked into my stricken face; I couldn't read what he was feeling – if anything. "So that's it, is it?" I said unsteadily. "After five years, you just walk away. It's that easy, is it?"

He stood, bag in hand. "No... No, it's not that easy. But it's not working for me. Not right now. Look, I'll be in touch... soon... see how I feel when I've had some time..."

I followed him downstairs and stood in the doorway as he opened his car to put his bag on the passenger seat, get in and drive off without looking at me.

I stood stock-still, lips trembling, staring at the empty street until I became aware that someone was talking to me. "Lucie? Sweetheart, are you okay?" It was one of my delightful neighbours who was peering into my face, looking very concerned.

"I... I..." I couldn't get any words out and turned away but instead of mine, found myself being steered through their front door.

Bart, Barthélemy to give him his proper name, came from a French father and an English mother so was equally at home in either country. He and his husband Edgar, had moved in next door about eight years ago, shortly after they'd married down in Brighton. Bart was tall, fair haired and green-eyed with a commanding presence, a wide smile and a wonderfully infectious laugh. Ed wore his thinning hair very short, had the most beautiful hazel eyes; bold and despite his wonderfully bold and eccentric clothes sense, was a little more reserved. It was hospitality work and their love of theatre that had brought them to Stratford; as a supplement they also operated Airbnb so occasionally I'd have an extra car on my drive. Once, Richard hadn't been able to get his silver 4-wheel drive off the road and, much to my embarrassment, had caused quite a kerfuffle about it; ever since then 'the boys' as I'd come to affectionately refer to them, had opted to give him a wide berth. However, the three of us had hit it off from the word go – they were a lovely couple and great neighbours. We gladly looked after each other's cats when away and, all of us being avid foodies, had happily shared many a barbeque on warm summer evenings.

I found myself on their comfortable blue sofa with an espresso in one hand and a brandy in the other. They looked at me. "Well?" That was almost in unison which made my lips curve upwards ever so slightly. So, taking a deep breath, I told them what had just happened.

Apart from the odd "No!", "Oh my God...", "Really?" and "Fucking hell!", they sat in silence as I talked. When I'd finished there was quiet for a few moments. The coffee and brandy had disappeared and had been swiftly replaced. I refused to join them for lunch, promising I'd be okay but that I needed to get home to cry. "If you're going to ugly-cry then we'll let you go." Ed's smile was warmly sympathetic.

Even as I closed my door behind me, I felt hot tears coming and cried for what seemed like hours. I wandered around, not knowing what to do, but hoped by moving I might be able to leave some of the heartache behind me. As I stumbled from room to room, I continued to cry in disbelief and grief. I lost count of the number of times I picked up the phone to call or text him but each time, managed to stop myself. I had some pride left – not a lot admittedly, but enough not to sabotage what was left of my self-respect.

Eventually I was all cried out, left with only the odd hiccupping sob. I stripped the bed unable to bear the thought of breathing in his scent when I tried to sleep. I slung the linen through the hottest wash I could twice before spraying the damp washing with my perfume so that all I would smell was me. Exhausted though I was, I barely slept that night.

The next morning while making my usual tea, I looked around the kitchen and noticed the almost-full bottle of Southern Comfort. I unscrewed the top and very slowly poured the contents trickle down the sink. I knew I was being wasteful and that Bart and Ed would have happily given it a home, but seeing it drain away felt sooooo good. I smashed the empty bottle into the sink, hearing with surprisingly intense pleasure the sound of breaking glass. I took Richard's favourite blue mug and banged it against a green one I'd never liked so both shattered. I ripped the red roses he'd bought me apart, not feeling the thorns piercing my hands and while I did all this, I cried in anger and bitterness, because I was seeing more and more clearly, I'd wasted my time, my love, and been taken for a fool.

What I absolutely couldn't get my head around was the cold-heartedness of how he'd behaved; the lulling me into a sense of false security, the gifts, the pretence of loving me – this hadn't been a spur-of-the-moment decision, this had been carefully thought out and executed. And, whilst disbelieving pain still ripped through me, anger was there too, tinged with contempt – over the coming days and weeks, that helped a lot.

Chapter 3

D espite knowing deep down that it was probably
for the best, the next few weeks were dreadful
– so much worse than I could ever have imagined.
As it slowly sunk in that Richard was probably never
going to be in touch, the whole sorry affair turned
into unfinished business so I was hardly ever free of
the many 'what if' thoughts that kept crashing into
my head. After his 'I'll be in touch… soon…' that
final Sunday, it weirdly felt like I was being punished
for a crime I knew I hadn't committed but still felt
guilty about. Ridiculously, I was on tenterhooks most
of the time and whilst I managed to cope with all
my booked-in work, the times I wasn't occupied I
just cried or talked to friends unendingly. 'What an
arse', 'selfish bastard', 'you deserve so much better'
and 'what the actual fuck?' were some of the more
memorable comments, all serving to reassure me that
almost certainly we were never meant to be. Memories
of the many negativities in our relationship, perhaps
unsurprisingly, had vanished as had the anger that had
initially kept me going.

One evening Carrie came round, insisting on
taking me out for a curry. Once there we decided to

share so ordered three starters – a pakora of crispy cabbage and onion, a crab cake served with sour lime chutney that made my mouth pucker, and a piece of chicken breast that had been marinated in creamed garlic and fennel infused yoghurt, all washed down with icy Cobra beer.

As we ate, we talked – mainly about me I have to say.

"I mean, why come back if he was going to do that?" I asked plaintively, it was an evening when I was feeling particularly sorry for myself.

"Fuck knows." Carrie was never one to hold back. "But you know he left simply because he was shagging someone else who happened to have more money than you…" That made sense.

"And actually…" To my surprise, Carrie looked uncomfortable. "I wasn't going to tell you, not while you were trying so hard to make it work, and it's possible I might have been mistaken – but I don't think so…" She was now looking upset. "I don't suppose you remember. It was ages ago. We'd gone shopping you and I, and ended up at the Boathouse, Richard had arrived early and rang to say he'd join us for a drink." I remembered; it had been shortly before their awful argument, my toes still curled with embarrassment whenever I thought about it. "Well, I went to say goodbye and when I put my hands on his shoulders, he groped my tits…" It had to be admitted she had the most stupendous boobs, in fact Richard had commented on them more than once. "I moved out of range straightaway, well as soon as I'd realised what he was doing. I mean, I couldn't believe it – that he'd do it at all and have the brass neck to do it in front of you? I'm so sorry Lucie." She looked as I sat with my mouth open. I wanted to say 'are you sure?' but didn't – I knew she wouldn't have said anything unless she was quite sure. "It all happened so fast, I wondered if I'd imagined it but… well, I know I hadn't. I didn't tell you at the time but it made me very worried when you went on seeing him. I guessed he never told you and I know if you'd seen anything you'd have said, so I just let it go." She paused thoughtfully. "I know it hurt you but truly it was a relief when we had that spat, so that I could justify not seeing him again." I sat, appalled that she'd been carrying this for so long but understood why she'd not told me.

We ate for a few moments in silence while I came to terms with her revelation.

"I think the very worst thing was the farewell fuck," she said thoughtfully. "I mean, who the hell does that? It's perverse, that's what it is." She wrinkled her nose. I told her of an earlier thought of dipping a treacherous cock in a bucket of bleach, which made us laugh a lot, a tremendously healing moment.

I'd booked in for one of my regular hair appointments and as I sat in the chair, having colour combed through I talked to Ricky, my wonderful stylist. He listened patiently to my story and stood with his mouth open as I recounted everything.

"What a bastard…" He poured us mint tea while my blonde streaks 'cooked'. "So, what are you going to do with that?" Rather disdainfully, he pointed to the 'commitment' ring that, for some reason, was still on my pinkie. I shrugged. "If it were me, I'd sell it." He looked again. "Mind you, it doesn't look like it's worth much." That's not very nice I thought.

A couple of days later it was time for my regular manicure so turned up wearing the brightest lipstick I could find in my messy makeup box. I decided to treat myself to a pedicure at the same time as Leigh had the time so chose slapper red for both hands and feet. It didn't matter that I usually wore closed-in shoes, just knowing my toes looked as pretty as my hands was enough to make me feel good.

Naturally I told her all about Richard's abrupt departure. After the usual 'Oh my Gods' and 'No!' her comment of, "Well, at least you can ease up on waxing your legs," made me laugh so hard I almost cried and through hiccupping laughter, had to admit that was a real positive to being a singleton once again, however small.

As I strode out, I heard a wolf whistle that made me smile even though it probably wasn't meant for me.

I stopped for a coffee at a café in the market square. As it was fairly warm, I sat outside, happily people-watching. I was feeling calm and relaxed until a sparkle on my left hand attracted my attention. I looked down – there was the 'commitment' ring. Do it now – right now – I thought as I stood up decisively.

I walked down a side street to a small jeweller I knew of and pushed the door open. It was a short conversation. "I'm sorry Madam – I'm afraid it's not something we're interested in." Apparently, the stones were fake, nice fakes but fake nonetheless, and it was gold-plated. I really didn't know whether to laugh or cry. After thanking the rather embarrassed assistant, I dropped the ring down the nearest drain – I couldn't think of anything better to do with it. I'd have to tell Ricky on my next appointment, I knew what his reaction would be and smiled at the thought.

One morning as I relaxed on the sofa, sipping a cup of tea, I looked around critically in the bright sunshine and realised the living room was looking decidedly shabby, it had been years since the place had been painted – and it was showing. Much as I loved the end result, I'd always hated the disruption of decorating so used the least little excuse to put it off.

Another dear friend, Anita, rang me that evening. I first met Anita at a National Childbirth Trust evening when we were both pregnant with our respective daughters. She was petite, wore her dark hair in a sharp bob, had the most amazing pale creamy skin and a ready smile that showed her beautifully even teeth. Thank goodness, our girls had got on very well from babyhood onwards so it was easy for us to continue our initial friendship. She was another one who had a husband with a wandering eye, so had divorced him after his third affair, when her children were quite little. However, she'd then met Jeff, a really considerate, agreeable man, in the school playground, not long after Alex had died, and married him a year later. All those years on they were still happily married.

I'd happened to bump into him at the supermarket very early on in their relationship. "Anita's having to work late," he'd explained. "Thought I'd just get a few of her favourite bits and bobs for dinner." He'd smiled his open smile. Now that, I'd thought as I watched him wander away is, most definitely, a keeper. I'd been proved right.

While we were chatting, I mentioned I was vaguely thinking of sprucing up the sitting room. "I love painting. You get the colour you want and I'll come over and help."

"Really?" I couldn't believe my luck.

"Really." As we said our goodbyes, we agreed that the end of the month was best for her.

Shortly afterwards, the phone rang again, it was Carrie checking up on me. "I'm okay. Really. I'm making sure every day's better and better…" and after I told her the story of the ring which made her laugh derisorily, I went on to tell her about my soon-to-be-smartened-up sitting room.

"I'd be more than happy to lend a hand – I really enjoy decorating. Why don't you get a few tester pots and try out some colours? And then maybe change your cushions." Carrie regularly transformed her house by moving furniture and pictures around, and changing her cushions which meant she never got bored with her space, a talent I'd long admired.

I visited our local DIY store at the weekend and bought a selection of tester pots, ranging from shades of blue and green to yellow, pinks and even a red – mainly for fun but just in case something I hadn't considered might just work. It was a bright morning that Sunday so I decided to make a start. I opened five of the pots I'd bought and started to dab a little patch on the wall but then, for some reason, Richard came crashing into my mind. Thoughtfully, slowly I painstakingly painted the word 'cheat' in large green letters opposite the fireplace. 'Despicable' in pale blue, 'fucker' in yellow and 'disloyal' in a darker shade of green followed. I stood, breathless, staring at what I'd just done. I was just about to paint over my handiwork when I heard the front door bell.

Carrie stood in the sunshine with a laden carrier bag in her hand. "I fancied a bacon buttie, so here I am." She held up a shopping bag.

"Carrie – lovely to see you. I can't think of anything nicer. Come on in."

"So, you trying out some colours in the sitting room?" Carrie asked through a mouthful of bacon.

I nodded. "I have indeed. Want to have a look?" I couldn't stop smirking.

We stood in silence for a few minutes as Carrie surveyed the graffitied walls. "Well, I don't know..." She looked at me with something akin to admiration.

"Want to contribute?" I held out a pot of dark pink.

"I'd love to, but just the one. This is your story." She painted a large blue 'cruel' just above the yellow 'fucker'. "Hey, amazingly satisfying, isn't it?" She giggled and I joined her until we were both helplessly laughing. It felt so good to share that moment with her,

After she left, I took down the remaining pictures and stared at the empty walls. The room looked sad and unloved. Not for long though, I said to myself as I pensively opened more tester pots and painted 'liar', 'untrustworthy', 'sneaky' and 'coward' in different colours. To my bewilderment, I wept as I did so. True and cathartic it might have been but it hurt so much to know that I'd given my love to a selfish, traitorous and misogynistic man who'd been happy to deceive me for a long, long time.

I'd been continuing to paint up different colours during the week so many more words had been added – 'prick', 'despicable', 'unfair', 'arse', 'dishonest' and 'selfish' now adorned the walls, each one being accompanied by bitter tears. Sunday morning saw 'shallow', 'crass', 'arrogant', 'unkind', 'heartless' and 'mendacious' – I'd had to check the spelling of that one before daubing it up. I sat in my oddly-decorated room cupping a hot drink, staring at the walls while yet more tears made my coffee salty.

Even though, as I knew I would, I'd eventually settled for a safe pale cream so had bought a large tin, a roller and a couple of brushes ready for the weekend, I'd also bought more tiny tester pots so that evening 'pathetic', 'tosser', 'egocentric', 'hurtful', 'wanker' and 'condescending' joined all the rest. This time I didn't cry. Reflecting on what Carrie had told me drove out any lingering sorrow and disappointment of lost love.

Early the next morning I opened the last tester pot and painted 'cunt' in big red letters above the fireplace. I ate some fruit while staring round the room, now wanting to see the words gone.

Carrie arrived just after nine thirty and as I made tea, she looked at the walls and nodded appreciatively. "Excellent Lucie. Couldn't have put it better myself."

Ten minutes later Anita was reading the walls. "Oh... my... God..." I wasn't sure whether she approved or not until she broke into giggles. "Well, you certainly said it loud and clear, didn't you?"

I nodded. "In the beginning it really hurt, but the last few felt wonderful. This one especially..." I pointed at my final red daub. Anita laughed and shook her head in disbelief.

"Before we start though," Anita was adamant, "you have to paint out all these words – that's your job. We're not doing that, are we?" She looked at Carrie who nodded emphatically.

"Absolutely not. We're going to watch you get rid of each and every one." She opened the large tin of paint, poured a little into a plastic tray and handed me the smallest brush there was. "Off you go then."

And they both sat back as slowly and deliberately I painted out every word. And as I did so, I said it out loud as it disappeared. I left 'cunt' til last and, as I watched the red paint vanish under the elegant cream, I let out a sigh of relief – as far as was possible, the last five years were gone.

Chapter 4

Work was nearly always on my mind. True I had my teachers' pension but that didn't really go close to covering everything, so I was always on the lookout for potential opportunities. Truth to tell, I loved it. I loved the actual work and equally loved the cut and thrust of finding it; it kind of gave me an adrenaline rush that kept me on my toes. I certainly didn't want a full-time commitment, but for so much of my life I'd been defined by how I earned a living – a habit far too hard to break.

One morning I read an email from an agency I'd registered with some time ago. Apparently, there was a local sixth-form college wanting a work experience/careers co-ordinator, as theirs was off on long-term sick leave and might this be something I might be interested in? Yes, as it was right up my street it certainly would be, I emailed back. Later that afternoon, a Bryan Haynes, acting Head of Maths who'd been taking on this role along with his normal teaching and admin duties, called me. "I've done quite a lot already," he explained, "but I really don't have the time and frankly I don't feel I'm doing the kids justice, never mind what the companies expect from us."

That I could well understand so the following morning saw me suited and booted, sitting in Bryan's office as we discussed what he saw as necessary. It was very obvious he was buckling under the strain of juggling far too many and diverse things to do. "The trouble is there just aren't enough hours in the day." I knew exactly what he meant and nodded sympathetically. He appeared older but I would have laid bets that he was only in his early forties. He looked drained and careworn; his grey-flecked hair almost blending with the grey of his suit; it was obvious he was running on pretty close to empty. He made it very clear that he was only too delighted I'd turned up as we chatted about what was needed. After an hour it had all been agreed. I would take on the role for twenty hours a week on a flexible basis. How perfect I thought as I drove away.

And that was only the beginning. Over the next few weeks, I was contacted by several other people – some previous clients and some who'd, very flatteringly, been recommended to get in touch. I pitched for every bit of work I could and happily, many of the outcomes were positive. Of course, I was delighted on but all too often, much to my irritation, a sneaky little thought that I wished Richard could see my busy success crept into my head.

Although friends reassured me it was only natural after such a relatively long relationship, Richard's betrayal and the nature of his leaving still hurt – less and less with every passing day it was true, but nonetheless even if it was just my pride, it still hurt.

One afternoon, when sitting in Anita's sunny garden and talking about being dumped yet again, I knew just why he kept haunting me. It was his 'I'll be in touch soon' that had stuck in my mind like a broken record, making me jump every time I heard the phone ring or a text ping through. That was the bit that continued to feel like unfinished business and that was the bit that seemed so unnecessarily callous. "So why on earth would you ever let someone who did that to you back in your life?" Anita had asked.

As often was the case, Jeff had left us to talk alone. He was a kind man, with thick greying hair, a ready smile, favouring open-neck shirts and baggy sweaters above all else. His most beguiling feature was that he was hugely respectful of Anita's space; in fact, he was the nearest thing to Alex in that he was never afraid of listening, admitting that he might be wrong and empathising – somewhat rare qualities in a man I'd always felt. He was a wonderful listener, his advice usually being sensible, balanced and helpful – a few of us had labelled him an almost-honorary-woman, high praise indeed.

We'd been talking for some time when we saw Jeff carrying out a tray on which there were three slices of excellent fruit cake along with tea refills. He sat, silently listening for a few moments. "I'm surprised at you Lucie, I really am." Anita and I stared at him. "He was never right for you, was he? Well, I didn't think so. You've got to stop going on about it though – it's not doing you any good." He smiled. "And frankly, I'm wondering if it's injured pride as much as anything else that's keeping you in this loop of self-pity." He looked at our nonplussed faces. "Just my two pen-orth – that's all…" Jeff was a man of few words but when he spoke, it was best to listen as, more often than not, it turned out that he was spot-on. This time was no exception.

A couple of weeks after Richard's departure, Carrie had persuaded me to join her at a Zumba class, held in a local church hall every Thursday evening. It was only an hour and a half she said, but the first time I went with her, all too quickly it became glaringly obvious just how unfit I was. I managed the first couple of dances but after that I found myself struggling more and more, eventually having to sit out while I watched the others. Another girl joined me and we ruefully commiserated with each other on our mutual struggles.

As the class drew to a close, someone suggested we go for a drink. What an excellent suggestion I thought so joined them. That after-exercise gathering became our norm over the next few weeks, and as with many groups of women, we quickly started to share confidences.

Although many were married or in settled relationships, there were a few of us singletons and our tales of dating and online fiascos combined with marital mishaps kept everyone amused.

Single Sara had been busy that last weekend. "He was a real lulu…" She looked pensive. "On his profile, it said he'd been divorced for three years so I'd assumed he'd be over it but all he could do was talk about his ex-wife ALL the time. It didn't matter what I said, he managed to bring every comment straight back to her. It really got to me; I mean it was so rude. After about an hour I'd had enough so after asking him why he was in a dating website – he said he wanted a relationship but it was so obvious all he wanted was to get her back – I made my excuses and left."

"At least she was his ex." I'd suddenly recalled a date I'd had a year or so before meeting Richard. "There was this man I met ages ago. He seemed really nice, said he was looking for a long-term relationship, we seemed to have lots in common, so loads of boxes ticked. I met him and we really got on. We had a lovely dinner, good wine, it felt like there was a real spark… it was all going so well until…" I stopped and looked at the ring of expectant faces round me. "Until he said he was married…" There was a collective gasp. "Yup, he was married. He then asked if I would sleep with him and his wife…"

"Well?"

"I said no – well actually I said no thank you." Even in those circumstances, I'd remembered my manners – my parents would have proud of me. "He looked really hurt and surprised. I couldn't think of anything else to say so just stood up and walked out. What else could I do?" The shocked giggles showed their agreement.

The next week, Sara told us about her latest date. "I met this man last weekend for lunch. He was really good-looking, very well dressed, our profiles showed that we had a lot in common." We leaned forward anticipating this might be a story with a happy ending.

"Trouble was that every other word was 'fuck' which completely put me off." We wrinkled our collective noses.

Natalie had been very quiet but when asked how things were with her, she took a deep breath. "I'm waiting for Ross to leave his wife..." There was another, smaller, combined gasp. She looked slightly rueful. "Hey, it's not as easy or clear cut as people think. He married her because she was pregnant. She refused to have an abortion which really was what he wanted. He's been unhappy for a long time, but now they've got three kids now – so it's difficult."

"Three kids?" Bev repeated softly. I glanced at Carrie who raised her eyes heavenward.

"You have no idea how hard it is, loving someone who's trapped in a loveless marriage. He's been talking about leaving her for the past year or so but there's so much to consider..." Her voice faded and we sat quietly.

Later, Carrie and I sat in the cool of my garden, talking, mainly about Natalie. I knew how Carrie had felt throughout most of her marriage as, year after year, affair after affair had been admitted to and forgiven only for yet another one to come to light. It had taken her a very long time but eventually she'd decided enough was enough and, one acrimonious divorce later, was contentedly mostly single and very much in control of her own life. "It doesn't matter how you dress it up, cheating's just not okay," was her final comment on the subject. She was quite right.

An hour later we hugged our goodbyes, both glad and grateful for our friendship.

More stories ensued and, perhaps unsurprisingly, Natalie made another contribution. "I met this guy at the gym. He was hyper-fit and incredibly good-looking. He wasn't overly bright but one can't have everything." Long-married Bev looked slightly disapproving. "Anyway, muscly he might have been, but not where it counts." She crooked her little finger. We looked at her with raised eyebrows and she shook her head. "Useless. Too little, too fast…" Our laughter interrupted her. "And, very much more to the point, no imagination," she added with a wry smile.

"Imagination wasn't the problem with the last guy I went out with before Andy and I got together," Lauren said, looking lovingly at her newly-given engagement ring. "He got off on taking photos of me. He'd have me dress up in kinky little outfits and, after taking his snaps, we'd have really good sex. Anyway, one time he set up his camera and filmed us – then the little shit posted it on YouTube…" We gasped. "I didn't know he'd done it and was livid when I found out. Luckily, it wasn't our faces he'd focused on but even so…"

Inevitably Sara had gone on another first date. "It's not that I think appearance is everything," she said plaintively. "But I do think one should make a bit of an effort, at least the first time you meet someone. Don't you?" We all nodded. "I mean we're expected to put lippie on…" She took a deep breath. "Well, I'd been talking to Bill for a couple of weeks and was happy to meet up for a coffee. You know it was quite hot last weekend?" We nodded again as she curled her lip. "Short sleeved Hawaiian-style shirt. Baggy shorts. Long diamond-patterned dark socks – and brown strappy sandals. That was bad enough but then he spent most of his time talking to my tits. Needless to say, I didn't stay long…"

"I was on holiday on Greece with my niece," Briony said as our laughter subsided, it was the first time she had contributed but her story was equally show-stopping. "We were having a really lovely time, looking at those fabulous Greek ruins, lazing around by the pool…" She paused so we urged her on. "Well, this very attractive chap came over. He was a bit young for me…" She had a faraway look in her eyes. "Anyway, he chatted me up and I was beginning to think 'oh well, why not?' so agreed to meet up with him later for a drink. I was getting ready when April came in – my niece…" she added as we raised our collective eyebrows interrogatively. "I told her that I'd met this man. She said she'd also met someone who was nice but much older than her. We were comparing notes but it was only when she mentioned he was missing the top part of his middle finger that we realised it was the same man. So, we decided we'd both turn up together." She giggled. "I had to admire his bottle… he bought us both a drink and said that if we fancied continuing the evening, he'd be delighted." She refused to be drawn any further on her story but we suspected his offer most probably had been refused.

Samantha had joined us after a few weeks away from Zumba. She seemed to have an inner sadness but the last couple of stories had made her smile. "I was on a dating site recently and started messaging this man who lived in Spain. He was really insistent we Skype so eventually I agreed and one day we got together." She looked at us. "You know when you're pretty sure someone's jerking off?" We grinned and nodded. "Well, there we were talking and I could see his arm moving. It was funny in one way and really gross in another so, as soon as I'd realised what he was doing, I said something like 'I can see you've got your hands full' and logged off." By this time, we were laughing helplessly as we visualised the picture. "He called me a few more times but I never replied. I just couldn't."

"This man contacted me ages ago," I said. "He called himself talktalktalk. His profile looked very interesting and we exchanged a couple of really nice emails before I gave him my number. He had the most wonderful voice – made you just melt. But there was a drawback… of course there had to be…" I paused for effect. "He wanted phone sex. Wouldn't Skype, wouldn't meet. He was okay with phone sex or even text sex but that was it. It's not that I mind phone sex…"

There were little squeaks from one or two who clearly weren't sure about the concept of phone sex. "Don't knock it till you've tried it," Natalie said, at which I chuckled.

"Well, if we're talking about phone sex…" Lily said at which we paid immediate attention. She smiled inscrutably. "With three kids all under five, it was impossible for me to get any work. So, of course I stayed home but took in bits and bobs of ironing to earn that little bit more." Most of us knew what she meant about having to turn one's hand to different things to bring in money and nodded sympathetically. "Craig was working really hard and decided to do a couple of extra shifts at night. Frankly, after having the kids all day I found just watching TV pretty boring after a while. I'd noticed an ad in a women's magazine that someone was looking for telephone operators working from home and thought that might be ideal. And..." She paused and looked at us archly. "Turned out it was a telephone sex line. Quite well paid too so I thought – why not? It was really good fun, actually I quite enjoyed it – know what I mean?" We sniggered. "It was all going nicely; I was managing to save some money and was going to surprise Craig with a weekend break – God knows he needed it, or so I thought. So, there I was working one night, when another call came through – and it was that little shit... Craig..." she added as we looked puzzled. "It was obvious he didn't know it was me. And anyway, he wanted it over fast so I played along." She took a deep breath. "When he got home that next morning it was like usual, he said hello to the kids, had breakfast with us and then went to bed." She looked pensive. "I never did surprise him with a holiday. Bought myself some fabulous boots instead..."

By this time, I'd decided that our after-exercise gossip made the exertion almost worthwhile so continued eagerly looking forward to my Thursday evenings.

One time, when we were discussing the merits of different dating sites, Gillian, who'd been quiet for some time, joined in. "Oh, I couldn't use one of those." Some of the group smiled; it was clear Gillian was well into her seventies.

"Why on earth not?" Natalie sounded slightly mocking. I frowned at her.

"Well, I don't have a computer." She looked at us, breaking into a wide smile. "And anyway, I'm seeing someone." She raised an eyebrow as she noticed Natalie's surprise. "Keith's a lovely man. We have great times but he keeps talking about us moving in together and I really don't want that. The last thing I want to do is hurt him but I just couldn't share my home on a full-time basis. We see each other about four times a week. Usually, he stays over and occasionally I go to his – that's quite enough for me."

"So, affairs of the heart never stop, do they?" I asked.

"Not if you don't want them to, no." I smiled at her and she winked back, I'd really warmed to her.

Debbie told us about a friend of hers. "She walked out on her cheating husband and left him to it with his girlfriend. One day she went back to the house while they were away in the Maldives for two weeks and, very carefully, she planted some spring bulbs in the lawn." We all looked puzzled. "Six months later the bulbs sprouted to spell 'bitch' and 'cheat' in the middle of the garden." We giggled. "But she also sprinkled the shag pile carpets with fast growing grass seed, watered them and turned the heating up. It's amazing how fast grass can grow in a fortnight." Clearly this was a woman who liked her revenge to be served very, very cold.

"Darren and I were taking a week out in Mykonos," Sunita said as our laughter died away. "One evening, we were having drinks on the rooftop balcony. It was so beautiful up there... it was very, very late, no-one else was there, we were feeling romantic and started making out. Well, one thing led to another and I ended up bent over a table..."

"And?" we demanded as she stopped.

She smiled sweetly. "It was amazing. But the next morning we went to the dining room and just as we finishing breakfast, the manager came over and asked if we realised there were CCTV cameras all over the hotel, including the rooftop balcony. I was mortified, especially as when he turned to leave, he looked at Darren, winked and said 'good show sir'. I think Darren was so pleased at the 'good show' he forgot to be embarrassed."

There was a brief pause as more drinks were brought over.

"So, who likes chocolate?" Alyssa asked. All of us nodded, some more enthusiastically than others. "Okaaaaay then..." She smiled teasingly. "I've not been seeing Sean for that long. I really like him; he might even be THE one. Know what I mean?" We nodded again. "We've not moved in together – yet – so I thought I'd spice things up, just to encourage him along the way... So, I bought some body chocolate and smeared it on the bits I thought might interest him... anyway, there I was, lying on the bed – I'd bought a brown towel, no point in ruining the sheets..." Our laughter threatened to drown her out. "All he said

when he saw me was 'but I've just started a diet'..."
In answer to our amused demands as to whether he'd
been enticed to break his diet, she simply smiled coyly,
saying, "What do you think?" and refused to be drawn
any more on the subject.

"Let me tell you about a friend of mine," Gillian
said after our laughter had subsided. "A few years ago,
her husband suddenly died of a heart attack and she
then found out he was on the verge of bankruptcy.
She'd not worked for years but managed to find
something part-time which allowed her to hold onto
the house by her fingertips. Anyway, she met this
very nice man who, after a while, confessed that he
liked to be dominated. You know – being handcuffed,
spanked, ordered about, that kind of thing. She was
very nervous about it but gradually did as he asked.
Apparently, she's pretty good at it too – he said so
anyway..." We sat in spellbound silence. "They were
very happy but, for all sorts of reasons, decided not to
stay together. But of course, she still needed to earn
money. Having been told she was a great mistress,
she decided to change her job..." she paused. "She's a
dominatrix now. Makes a very good living I understand
– she's just had a lovely big conservatory built on the
back of the house"

That was, we all agreed, one of the better jaw-
dropping stories until Natalie piped up. "Well girls,
I might be able to top that." We fell silent in eager
anticipation. "I dated this man for a while and very
quickly saw that he was like your friend's guy – liked
to be dominated. I'd never done it before but thought

– oh well, in for a penny, in for a spanking." She was interrupted by laughter. "It gets better. He liked to be handcuffed, gagged, whipped – that sort of thing. But then he asked me to dress up as a schoolgirl…"

"Oh no!" Bev's hand flew to her mouth.

"And pee on him. Well, for me that was a step too far so I said no. He said if I didn't, we were over and he'd find someone who would."

"And what did you do?" Gillian asked.

"I put my knickers back on and left him to it. Never saw him again. For all I know he's still handcuffed to that bed…" We were all laughing so much that other guests at the bar stopped talking and looked round at us, but we couldn't stop and it was on that show-stopping note we said our goodbyes.

By the time classes took a break of three weeks we realised that, for relative strangers, we were becoming a supportive group of good friends.

There was just one fly in my ointment. At the sixth-form college, I had to work closely with Bryan, but he had one propensity that I really didn't like – he tended to tell off-colour jokes. It wasn't that I was a prude, far from it, but had always disliked schoolboy smuttiness along with a penchant for lavatory humour – it made my toes curl in embarrassment and was, to my mind, entirely inappropriate for the staffroom. It ended up that I did my best to avoid being alone with him, and I knew from the odd comment that other members of staff, both male and female, felt much the same.

It had also become obvious that he wanted us to be more than just good working colleagues, asking me out several times. Questionable jokes apart, he was a bright, interesting man. And now the strain of multiple roles had been lifted, he was showing a more light-hearted approach to life in general and work in particular. He could have been nice for someone, but certainly and especially so soon after Richard's abrupt departure, I was in no way ready for anything more than a working relationship. And I didn't fancy him – not one little bit even though he was reasonably good looking. Irritated about what he thought were witticisms, no spark AND absolutely the wrong time I told myself as yet again I refused the suggestion of going out for a drink one evening.

Rather sadly it came as a real relief when the long-term-sick co-ordinator was told she could start coming back on a phased return. I spent a few days bringing her up to speed with what I'd been doing and assured her I'd be more than happy to stay in touch if there was anything we hadn't covered in the handover.

For the final time I said a polite 'thank you but no thank you' to Bryan, shook hands firmly and left. He did email me once more but I didn't reply. And that was that I thought as I firmly pressed the delete button – enough really was enough.

Chapter 5

After my foray into decorating, I'd spent time in a spot of decluttering, managing to fill three black sacks, ready for taking to a local charity shop. It was one morning, as I sat outside in the weak sunshine with my customary cuppa, that I looked around and had to admit the back garden was decidedly lacking, Bart had said as much the last time they'd come over and he was quite right. It wasn't shabby exactly, just unloved and rather unkempt. What I knew about gardening could have been written on the back of a very small postage stamp – my beloved Alex had been the one with green fingers whereas I was all thumbs so, ever since his death, I tended to do the absolute minimum to keep on top of things. Richard's occasional forays into my wilderness had made more of a difference than I'd care to admit, was it that I was missing more than him I wondered.

"Pots," I murmured to myself. "And herbs." I loved cooking so tending to a few herbs surely wouldn't be that much of a hardship to look after – would they? And perhaps a climber or two to soften the fences, that'd look lovely. I felt myself getting quite excited at the prospect and went inside to get dressed, I'd recently taken to spending non-working mornings lounging around in my dressing gown.

Despite the cloudless skies, it was a little chilly so I pulled on black jeans, black ankle boots, and a belted long white shirt topped by my ankle-length red cardigan with a black and red scarf. Even though it was only a trip to a garden centre, ever since making my promise to Ricky, I made an effort to look presentable every time I left the house – and it worked. I'd felt so much better since then.

The nearest garden centre was only a few miles out of Stratford. There were several independent little shops tucked away at the back so I happily looked at those first and bought the most beautiful bright orange bag that looked surprisingly like a Lulu Guinness one I'd recently seen online and been lusting after but really couldn't afford. It was a relative snip – far too good to walk away from.

In my pleasure at discovering such a find I'd almost forgotten the real purpose of my visit. With a determined sigh I fetched a trolley and started looking. I found the pots and was stunned at the cost of some of them but then saw some others that were almost as nice and loads cheaper. I braced myself to pick one up – the others I liked so far were incredibly heavy – but this one was as light as a feather. I would never have guessed from the look of it that it was plastic but there it was. Less than half the price, looked great and easy to move. I picked up three, identical design but different sizes. My favourite herbs of the moment were rosemary, mint and thyme so that was my next job.

Having selected three robust-looking plants, I started to look for a couple of climbers which was a much harder task. There were so many – from hydrangeas to clematis, roses to azaleas. I didn't find the labels much help either so looked around to find someone who might know what they were talking about. As always, there was no-one around so, rather impatiently, I pushed my trolley towards the building.

I noticed a tall, well-built man in a green tee-shirt fiddling around with some plants. "Excuse me." He totally ignored me. "Excuse me?" I raised my voice. He must have heard me but still nothing. I moved a little closer. "Excuse me…" I used my imperious voice; this time he turned round and smiled at me. He didn't ask if he could help, just stood there. "Are you busy? Or can you help?" By this time, I was quite cross.

He took a step towards me. "Yes… madam. How can I help you?"

And about time too I thought as I explained what I wanted. "And I don't know whether to go for hardy, semi-hardy or what it means if I do or don't." He was very good-looking, was dark with a few grey hairs at the temple, sported designer stubble which I'd always thought incredibly sexy, and striking café-au-lait skin.

As it turned out, he knew a lot about plants. He explained that some of the varieties of bamboo were not only beautiful but very fast growing. "It's best if you plant them in a big bucket and sink that into the ground; that'll keep the roots in check, otherwise it'll take over everywhere." I picked a slender bamboo with almost black stems and pale green leaves that was promised to be a fast grower and easy to look after. He was so helpful, I felt confident in asking for more. "What about roses?" What indeed? I selected an ice-white bush together with an old English gloriously deep yellow climber that was apparently named Graham Thomas in tribute to a leading garden designer and writer. I couldn't resist a vine for the fence at the back of the garden, the label said it would give spectacular autumnal colours of gold and orange.

"Well, thank you for all your help." He really had been very obliging; I'd quite forgiven him for his earlier rudeness.

"I hope you like them." He paused. "I'd be very happy to give you a hand planting them."

I drew myself up to my full height and was about to say most emphatically that he'd well overstepped the mark when a girl wearing a similar tee-shirt hurried over. "I'm so sorry to have kept you waiting Mr Moore. Your order hasn't arrived yet but it should be in in another week or so."

As she walked away, we stared at each other. "I'm very sorry… madam…" It was clear he was trying to keep a straight face. "But I really do know quite a bit about plants. Honestly…" The dimple in his left cheek was very attractive and his smile was nothing short of captivating.

I was mortified. "I'm so sorry. I thought… you're wearing the same colour tee-shirt and I thought… and, well…" Much to my relief he laughed. "Look, I'm very grateful for all your help, I really am. And I think the very least I can do is buy you a coffee, and probably a very large cream cake."

"That's very kind. I'd love to."

We sat in the café for well over two hours. He was incredibly easy company, smiled and laughed readily, and listened attentively when I talked. He had the slightest burr of a Somerset accent which made him very easy listening. His eyes were like pools of dark treacle and he had long, long eyelashes. When I said I had to go, he walked me to my car, loaded the pots and plants in and waved goodbye as I pulled out of the carpark. As I got home, I realised that not only did I not know very much about him apart from his love of gardening, our mutual taste in music, some of his travels and that, like me, he was an avid foodie, but that I'd given him my mobile number. I flipped from thinking he might be a serial killer to reflecting on his easy laugh, the way his face crinkled when he smiled and the merest tinge of grey at streaking his almost-black hair which was thick and very slightly too long; just the way I liked men's hair to be worn. I'd also noticed that the top part of his right middle finger was missing which, touchingly, made him seem strangely vulnerable.

I certainly hadn't expected to meet someone who had made my pulse beat that little bit faster. As I took the pots and plants through to my back garden, it stuck me that Richard hadn't had that effect on me for ages.

A few days later, I was driving home from a very productive meeting with a client and, feeling very pleased with myself, had a Queen CD on quite loud and was singing along to 'Don't Stop Me Now'. Before I'd set off, I'd dealt with an urgent email so my mobile was on the passenger seat next to me. I became conscious of an extra sound and, glancing down, saw there was an incoming call. A second glance showed that what was now a missed call was from a number I didn't recognise.

I got home, unloaded the car and went through to make myself a coffee which I sipped as I read through my notes. A loud meow interrupted my train of thought – there, circling round my feet, was Biba, my little black cat who, ever since kittenhood, had had the loudest voice of any cat I'd ever known.

It must have been about an hour later when my mobile rang again – same number as before. I picked up.

Two minutes later I was back in the car, driving as fast as I dared to a local vets' surgery. Once there, I was told Whispa, my beautiful fluffy ginger tom's story. He'd been hit by a car, just outside my house. Apparently, the driver was distraught and taken him to her vet who checked him for a microchip which was when they'd rung me before seeing what could be done for him. The car had hit him with what had seemed like a glancing blow but the damage was massive – broken back leg and tail, fractured pelvis, and considerable internal bleeding. He'd been given painkillers while the vet considered options.

I could barely speak through my tears but managed to ask to see him. He was in a terrible state, fur matted with dried blood and a kind of inward look in his eyes. He managed to look up and almost inaudibly meowed as I touched him tenderly. One of the nurses came through with his x-rays and, as I continued to gently stroke his head and shoulders, heard the vet's sympathetic voice outlining his prognosis. Operating was going to ferociously expensive with no absolutely guarantee of success – there was no question he'd have to lose his leg and probably his tail. His pelvis was shattered but there was an outside chance it could be pieced together, at this stage, it was impossible to tell the extent of soft tissue damage.

I gazed into my furry friend's amber eyes. "We have to give him a fighting chance." I looked at the vet pleadingly before turning to Whispa, kissing the top of his silky head and murmuring that he was to be a brave boy. I could hear him purring as he was carried out.

Being a brave boy didn't save him – he died on the operating table.

The next day I went to pick up Whispa's body and pay the vet who was compassionately sympathetic when I burst into tears yet again. As I carried the small box through the house and into the back garden, Bart and Ed were waiting for me. They'd already dug a neat little grave at the top of the garden by the fence and there we laid him to rest. On Bart's suggestion, we planted the yellow climbing rose over him so he'd be especially remembered every time the roses bloomed. It was very strange but throughout the whole little funeral and planting, their cat, Bon-Bon, along with Biba, joined us and they sat close together, silently watching. "They know," Ed said. We agreed with him, of course they were joining us in saying goodbye to a beloved friend.

Two days later a text pinged through. 'I was serious when offering my help to plant up but I guess you've done it by now. How are you? Isn't it my turn to buy you a drink and a bun? Sam' He'd put two smiley faces after his name. Sam…Sam? I remembered – Samarth Moore, the man I'd thought was an assistant at the garden centre. Why was I smiling and my tummy flipping?

I deliberately left it an hour or so before replying – mustn't look overly keen. 'You're quite right, all the planting's done and looking great. I guess it might just be! Lucie' I put one smiley face before the exclamation mark. A couple more texts later and I'd agreed to meet him for lunch, insisting that it be at the Boathouse; I'd always felt safe and comfortable there.

At two minutes after twelve thirty, I took a deep breath and strode in, head held high. Heaven knows why, but I'd spent some time in deliberating what to wear, eventually selecting my baby pink sweatshirt with a matching scarf, black jeans and black boots. Sam was already there, sitting at the very table that had been Richard's and my favourite. As I made my way towards him, I felt a sudden, albeit ridiculous, jolt of disloyalty but quickly dismissed that. He stood to greet me with a warm smile and leaned over to kiss my cheek lightly. I noticed he was wearing dark grey jeans with a pale grey shirt – unpretentiously stylish I thought, and smiled. "Lucie, how very good to see you. What would you like to drink?" I'd detected a hint of a slightly earthy, citrusy cologne when we'd kissed; I loved a subtle cologne on men.

"Sparkling water please. Ice, no slice." I'd decided to stick to soft drinks.

He ordered the same and smiled as we simultaneously picked up our glasses and raised them to each other. Initially I felt a little self-conscious but that faded once we started chatting. Within moments it felt just like we'd been at the garden centre.

This time we told each other more about ourselves. Sam explained he'd dropped out of university due to a nervous breakdown, partly triggered by too many recreational drugs; how brave to talk about that to a relative stranger I thought and looked at him with renewed respect. Preferring outside life, he'd worked as a handyman/gardener for a while and although he liked the freedom that gave, his overwhelming love of good food prompted him to go to catering college which he'd thoroughly enjoyed so he'd opted to stay in hospitality ever since. However, his fondness for all things horticultural had stayed with him which was why he'd been at the garden centre, buying plants for hanging baskets. "I'm part-owner of a couple of gastro-pubs so I get to cook and look after the gardens – best of both worlds. What's not to like about that?" What indeed I thought.

We shared an excellent board of fishy nibbles and warm pitta bread with some chips and salad on the side. Sam stayed on the sparkling water as did I. Time flew by – we didn't stop talking, listening, laughing. To my delighted surprise, I was feeling increasingly relaxed and at ease.

By mid-afternoon we were strolling across the bridge into town, having asked the Boathouse to keep our table as we'd decided to return for a snack later. We ended up in front of the Royal Shakespeare Theatre where we found a bench and sat, watching children feed the ducks and swans. I told him about Alex, my work and Susie, explaining that although I missed her, I was so glad she had the amazing opportunity to work in Italy and how happy I was that she'd met Patrizio. We talked more about gardening, when I told him about Whispa's yellow rose he said what a fitting tribute it was for such a special friend – I wasn't sure whether that was sincere or not, but certainly it was a kind thing to say. We went on, to my joy, to talk about food and recipes – it was obvious he knew a great deal about good food.

We returned to our table; this time I allowed myself a small gin and tonic as we looked through their evening menu and settled on their surf-and-turf board. "Just so we can share again," Sam had said with a soft smile. I adored sharing food, something that Richard had heartily disliked. I smiled back, revelling in the moment.

It was pitch-dark when Sam said he had to go. "Can I walk you home?"

I giggled – we'd moved away from water onto wine and I'd probably drunk a bit more than I should. "You can walk me to my car if you like."

He did. And after he'd opened the door for me, he held my face in both hands and brushed his lips against each corner of my mouth before kissing me with an intensity that took my breath away. "I've had the best day," he murmured. "We are going to see each other again, aren't we?"

"Oh, I think so... definitely..."

On the short drive home, I reflected on the last few hours which had been entertaining, interesting and delicious in equal measure – not to mention that gently insistent, oh-so sensual kiss. As I drifted off to sleep, my lips were curved into a smile...

Chapter 6

It was a text pinging through that woke me a little earlier than I'd have liked. 'Good morning Lucie, trust you slept well, I dreamed of you. Looking forward to seeing you again. Sam x'. I stretched luxuriously, showered, dressed and applied my makeup with care before sitting in the garden with my first cup of tea of the day.

I had to think. I liked Sam – probably a lot. Probably more than I'd care to admit even to myself. But I didn't really know much about him; that's easily remedied my little inner voice said. And I've only recently come out of a relationship; what's that got to do with anything the little voice asked. And he's obviously quite a bit younger than me; my little voice giggled – I knew what my neighbours would have to say on the subject, not to mention Carrie of course. I continued debating and arguing with myself. The real bottom line was – was I prepared to take a chance on the possibility of another relationship which opened the door to potentially more heartbreak? I sighed as I went in to make breakfast.

Over the past few weeks, Carrie had been nagging me, in the nicest possible way, to get back online to see 'what was around' as she put it. Her view was that dating was a bit like riding a horse – falling off was inevitable but the best remedy was to climb straight back on. "After all sweetie, you're not likely to bump into Prince Charming in the local supermarket, are you? And frankly you're not getting any younger – well, none of us are…" It had been at that point I'd firmly shushed her but knew she was right.

And then, out of the blue, almost literally I'd bumped into Sam. I couldn't wait to tell her…

I dropped her a text, inviting her for a post-work drink at mine. This time the drinks in the garden were a supermarket's own Bucks Fizz, a cheap but very palatable substitute to the real thing. She listened thoughtfully. "You like him?" I nodded. "You had fun?" I nodded again. "You like the way he kissed?" I nodded, reddening slightly. "And you say he's younger than you?" I reddened more. "How much younger?"

"Ten… fifteen… oh God, maybe even more…" Suddenly I was aghast as I realised just how much the age gap might be.

"Oh, for fuck's sake Lucie. Just go out, enjoy yourself, have fun…" She giggled at my shocked face. "It's not like you had that much fun with Richard, did you?" She was right. Apart from the odd flurry of impromptu excitement and pleasure, the last couple of years… longer if I was being brutally honest… had dwindled into a humdrum domesticity which he'd smilingly call his 'weekend oasis of calm' and which I now called blandly lacklustre same-old, same-old.

I checked with another couple of friends for their opinions. Anita urged caution as did Shona, but Marie who I'd once worked with a long time ago and been blissfully married to a man sixteen years her junior for well over twenty said much the same as Carrie.

Seemed like my misgivings were unfounded. Over the next few days Sam and I exchanged slightly flirty but entirely proper texts before we met up again, this time in a lovely place called the Trout in Wolvercote, a popular riverside pub just outside Oxford. He'd explained he had meetings with potential suppliers in the area and wondered if I minded the hour-long drive? Of course I didn't, I'd texted back enthusiastically; I really didn't, somewhere out of the norm was a welcome change.

Ever the girlie-girl, I chopped and changed between different outfits but eventually settled on a boho style maxi-dress topped with a lime-green wrap. I'd adored recently treated myself to of a pair flip-flop-type sandals with lots of glitter so wore those teamed with a cross-body bag of dark red that toned beautifully with one of the colours in the dress. I twirled in front of my mirror and nodded in satisfaction – I would do.

Sam had arrived before me and was sitting at a table on the terrace, overlooking the Thames where boats could be seen lazily chugging along. He rose as he soon as he saw me. He was wearing a crisp blue and white striped shirt with jeans and beautifully polished tan shoes – there was no doubt about it, I adored men who knew how to dress in a delightfully understated way. "What a great table," I exclaimed as we kissed hello. He was wearing the same cologne and this time I sniffed appreciatively, he returned the compliment by murmuring he loved my perfume.

I love the old-fashioned style so was delighted he waited for me to sit before settling himself down again. "I thought you'd rather be outside."

"Absolutely. It's far too nice an evening to be inside." I made myself comfortable.

"Perhaps you'd like a glass of bubbly?" We watched our waiter skilfully open the bottle and raised our glasses.

We sat for nearly an hour, sipping the ice-cold champagne, nibbling on a dish of delicious Pulgian olives, which reminded me of wandering through olives groves under the hot Italian sun many years ago. I suddenly thought how good it might be doing that with him and, for a brief moment, wondered if that might be a flash into the future. We chatted on, mainly about work and travel. And even though the night became quite chilly, the nearby heater kept us nicely toasty warm.

We read the Trout's extensive menu before we decided to share a baked camembert spiked with garlic and thyme accompanied by three wonderfully fresh-out-of-oven artisan breads; a soft and slightly crumbly sourdough with a brittle crust, a heavily olive-oiled yielding Italian focaccia topped with rosemary and sea salt, and some crispy little rolls that we were told were based on Chilean gluten-free marraquetas. All were excellent and accompanied the soft warm cheese beautifully.

I'd always adored sharing food so was in seventh heaven. We giggled as we mock-squabbled over the last morsels and mock-argued over what to eat and drink next. Truth to tell, the camembert was easily enough but when Sam suggested a cold beer to accompany a shared seafood platter, including lobster along with salad and a few chips, I greedily agreed.

I was swept back to my first proper 'dirty weekend' with Alex in Brighton when we'd feasted on fresh lobster and chips at a wonderful seafood restaurant tucked just behind the Brighton Pavilion. He'd chosen it in an effort to impress me, it was superb but terribly expensive, so much so that I'd had to slip him a tenner under the table. I think it was at that moment, seeing his confusion, when I'd fallen for him completely and utterly. When, many years later, we decided to return we'd been told that Bentleys had closed, and now only operated out of London.

"How does that sound?" Sam's voice broke into my reverie.

"Marvellous, couldn't be better," I assured him.

As we munched our way through gastronomic heaven, talking non-stop, I felt more and more comfortable with him.

The dessert menu was as comprehensive as the mains and, despite my protestations, we wavered for several minutes, before settling on what they called the House-Sharer. When it arrived, we knew we'd made the right decision as we sampled crème brûlée with cherries under a crackling sugar crust, a salted caramel chocolate pot that made my toes curl, a slice of meltingly scrumptious pear tarte tatin and an American-style ice-cream cookie sandwich. It was such a joy to talk about food and recipes, something I'd long loved doing but Richard never had. Yet again I was irritated with myself that I'd allowed him to insinuate himself into my mind and shook my head to get rid of him once and for all – after all, weren't comparisons odious?

As we finished our excellent coffee, I saw it was close to midnight. We'd been the last people on the terrace for some time but I could see the restaurant was now empty. He walked me to my car and as we said goodbye, found myself enfolded in a close hug when his unmistakable arousal became obvious. We kissed long and slow before gently drawing apart.

On the drive home I sang along to romantic ballads and thought of the way he laughed easily, smiled a lot and listened intently. It added up to an incredibly beguiling package. And he'd insisted to picking up the tab – that was so sweet; old-fashioned gentlemanly manners, something I really appreciated.

Naturally I sent Sam a little 'thank you' text when I arrived home but became increasingly puzzled when he didn't answer for two days. Maybe he didn't like me? Maybe he'd blocked my number? Maybe – the thought appalled me – he wasn't single even though he'd intimated he was. He hadn't explicitly said that though – had he? I really couldn't remember. I decided to let it go but then on the third day he called to apologise for not being in touch sooner. "It's been crazy busy. I'm so sorry but you know what work is." I knew what work was but equally the thought that it would only have been a matter of moments at most to send a text momentarily flashed into my mind. But it's not like he's your boyfriend or anything like that, I told myself. "Just give me a few days so I know what I'm doing, then we'll sort out getting together. That okay?" It had to be.

I was distracted from thinking about how my heart had skipped a beat when first hearing his voice, by a phone call from Di. I'd known Di for many years; we'd first met through a contract I'd been involved with, after which we found we got on very well, becoming fast friends. Disbelievingly I read, and then had to re-read her text – after just over three years in a job she'd painstakingly developed, she was being made redundant. I called her and after a brief chat when it was clear she'd been crying, we agreed I'd go to her's that evening.

I made a beef stroganoff to take with me along with a bag of washed leaves so she didn't have to bother about cooking and loaded it in the car along with a chilled bottle of Bucks Fizz and a large bunch of yellow roses.

Di was a minimalist – her house was immaculate with everything always in its right place. She was slim with cropped blonde hair and blue, blue eyes. At first, I'd been intimidated by her understated efficiency and orderliness but once I'd got to know her properly, appreciated her razor-sharp wit and sense of humour. Di's philosophy was once a friend always a friend and whilst we didn't see that much of each other, there was no question that, come any sort of a crisis, we were there for each other.

We sat in her beautiful grey and white sitting room and sipped our drinks. "Well, I didn't see that coming..." Di had been working for a very large company based in London, managing their many new recruits. I sat listening silently as she poured everything out – how after only three years she'd get precious little in redundancy, how worried she was as she'd only recently moved house, how long it had taken her to find this job and how anxious she was that she wouldn't find another one.

"Di, you know that things'll work out because somehow they always do. I know how scary this is. But you mustn't worry – one door closes, another door opens and all that sort of stuff..."

She smiled at my attempt to cheer her up, albeit by platitudes. "Well, at least I've got my three months' notice plus a tiny bit of redundancy so I can manage for a little while. I really thought this job was for keeps. I can't bear the thought of starting all over again."

"I know, I know." I'd been there and knew exactly how she felt. "It's a horrible feeling when you think you have something stable and suddenly discover you're on shifting sands." She nodded tearfully.

The stroganoff and salad went down very well and later, after the Bucks Fizz had been finished, we cosied down with a very large bowl of chocolate ice cream each. Di opened a bottle of wine but, knowing I was driving later, I moved onto lime cordial. "Oh, don't be silly Lucie. Have another drink. You'll stay, won't you?" I rang Ed, my lovely constant helping hand, who assured me they'd look in on Biba to make sure she was alright before I joined Di with another glass of wine.

It was well after midnight when we weaved our way upstairs. Di was squiffier than me but I was well on the way. We hugged affectionate goodnights and retired.

I woke to lashing rain and wrinkled my nose in displeasure. Never mind, I thought, it's not like I have to dash off to work and I knew Di had decided to take a day off anyway. I smelled bacon and toast and made my way downstairs to find her pouring orange juice and brewing coffee. We devoured her excellent bacon sandwiches and had taken ourselves into the siting room with fresh coffee.

"Now, tell me all about this new man of yours…" Di tucked her feet under her as I did the same. "He sounds nice," she said after I'd told her about how we'd met, our subsequent date and how different he seemed to be from Richard. Heaven knows why I had to mention Richard but he still bubbled up like an occasional itch I had to scratch.

I knew Di understood all too well how I felt. She'd lost her Henry to another woman a long time ago. They'd been together for over twenty years, working and living together, sharing some wonderful and amazing times. Di had begun to suspect something was wrong when Henry used work as an excuse to come home later and later, go to conferences and exhibitions, and generally be away from home more and more. Unsurprisingly he was having an affair. By the time Di had found out and kicked him into touch in a spectacular scene played out in her office for all to hear, it'd been rumbling on for well over a year.

"It's really odd how memories pop up sometimes, don't they?" Di's voice was reflective.

We sat in silence for a few moments. "When does the pain of being betrayed go away?" I knew I sounded child-like but really wanted to know.

Di laughed. "God knows. Me being cheated on was ages ago but sometimes, 'specially when I'm down, I remember how much Henry hurt me but hey… we just have to recognise that it's a shitty thing to do to someone who's meant to be your true love and who trusts you, and the people who do this are real shits – never worth what we give them. We deserve so much better than that. I have to say I'd rather be single for the rest of my life than tolerate that level of bad behaviour" She raised her cup. "Here's to us."

I raised mine and we solemnly sipped the now-tepid coffee.

We talked some more. "Don't suppose you fancy going away for a few days, do you?" I was surprised but delighted. Di and I had spent a couple of short breaks together and been great travelling companions but that had been… I suddenly occurred to me that the last time had been just before I'd met Richard.

I nodded thoughtfully. We spent the next couple of hours discussing where we might go. We settled on the last week of the school term so that we avoided the school holidays but couldn't manage to agree where. What we did arrange though was that Di would come to me for dinner next weekend after we'd had a chance to have an individual think before making a joint decision – we were nothing if not democratic in determining what to do.

The following Saturday I cooked a chicken and ham pie which, I was highly gratified to be told, was almost as tasty as Di's. High praise indeed, given that it was her recipe. After two glasses of rosé and much debate, we agreed on Northern France for our upcoming holiday. We'd spent time together in the Loire Valley but neither of us knew Brittany that well. Not too far but far enough we said, and not too expensive to get to – we both needed to be mindful of budget.

Di had recently treated herself to a soft-top car. Naturally I didn't begrudge her but was very envious so, when she suggested we use it for our trip, I was delighted to go along with her plan. I suddenly remembered one of Susie's school trips when her class visited that area. "Di, shall we stop off in Bayeux? I've always wanted to see the Bayeux tapestry and as we'll be so close…"

"You know, I've never seen it either," Di said thoughtfully, so that was agreed. We spent some time poring over maps to decide which ferry to book and where we'd stay. Despite the vagaries of Brexit, the ferry crossing between Dover and Calais still seemed the best, as it gave the most flexibility in terms of time, not to mention being the cheapest. We agreed to share the driving which thrilled me; I always enjoyed motoring and the thought of sweeping through the French countryside in Di's swish little silver Peugeot was very appealing. "Let's try and get to Calais early in the morning so we get to wherever for lunchtime." No sooner said than done, we were online booking the 0640 ferry which arrived at 0910. We then agreed to pre-book the first nights' accommodation nearer the time when we'd decided exactly where to visit and spent the rest of the evening talking about our soon-to-be travels. "It's just what I need," Di said. I nodded. It had been ages since I'd had a holiday, years in fact. I was more than ready for a change of scene.

Sam called, inviting me for lunch that Sunday at Sarastro's in London's Drury Lane as he was down south that weekend. "I'm seeing my gran in Slough but she'll probably have had enough of me by then, and I'll certainly be wanting to get out." He laughed as I sat stunned, wondering just how much younger than me he was. Best not to ask – certainly not on the phone anyway. We chatted a little longer when I admitted I'd never heard of Sarastro's, never mind been there. "You're going to love it," I was he assured.

I awoke to a warm and balmy Sunday morning with not a sign of a cloud in the sky so decided to wear a summer dress I'd recently treated myself to from a positive Aladdin's cave of a shop for the curvier woman. It was Italian, fine cream and dark blue stripes with a grandad-style collar and long sleeves I tended to wear pushed up to the elbow. The loose dropped waist made it an easy wear, ideal for a lunch date. I teamed it with blue ballet pumps and a cream and blue flowery scarf, and nodded at my reflection – that would do very nicely.

Trains were never that reliable on a Sunday so I decided to drive down to park at a little spot just by the Oval cricket ground which I knew well as Alex and I had watched innumerable matches much to his delight and my thinly disguised boredom – but then he'd partner me at bridge because I loved it and he didn't. Fair was only fair was our thinking. I took the tube to Leicester Square which was only a short step to Drury Lane where I saw Sam standing, waiting for me. This time he wore black jeans with a snowy white shirt, a grey waistcoat and highly polished dark tan shoes, he was continuing to impress me with his sartorial style. I was enveloped in a warm hug and as we strolled into the restaurant, I gasped, looking around at the opulent yet slightly dilapidated surroundings. "Isn't just the ultimate shabby chic?" he asked as we were shown to our seats.

"Fabulous. Just amazing."

"Now, I'm sure you want to go and freshen up." I was puzzled. "Just go to the ladies," he urged.

I headed upstairs and was met by faded but very explicit and beautifully erotic art adorning the walls. From what he'd said, Sam knew exactly what I was looking at – beautifully executed French-style murals of couples making love in different positions – as I made my way downstairs, I wondered what he'd been thinking in my absence.

"Well?" He looked amused as I took my seat.

"Well..." I echoed. "It's certainly a... different décor from the usual ladies." Ridiculously I felt my cheeks reddening.

"Lucie. I do believe you're blushing..." He chuckled which made me laugh before he went on to change the subject to talk about the menu. As always, I was more than happy to share so we started off with their mezze platter which consisted of two types of filled puff pastries, one with cheese, the other crammed with shrimp; a lemony hummus, yoghurt crammed with chopped cucumber and garlic, tiny kebabs, crispy rolls of paper-thin dough stuffed with cheese and parsley, and a Turkish style couscous salad, all served with thin slivers of flatbread accompanied by ice cold light beer.

"So how come you're such a foodie?" I was asked.

"Well, I've always liked eating – can't you tell?" I glanced down at myself semi-deprecatingly.

He shook his head and frowned. "Don't be silly – you're lovely." I only just restrained myself from batting my eyelashes.

"Thank you, kind sir." I smiled at him. "Well, I really enjoy cooking for and eating with people. Food and pleasure kind of belong together in my mind. As a child I used to watch my mother cook. She was amazing – she could create a great meal out of almost nothing – and frequently did. Our door was always open. I remember people sitting round our table eating and drinking and having a great time. I suppose that's what makes me want to create food that gets people smiling."

He nodded understandingly. "My gran's the most phenomenal baker; her cakes are still amazing but back in the day they were phenomenal. She used to make people's wedding cakes and stuff like that. As a kid, I'd help her – that's where it all started for me…"

As the table was cleared and we waited for our next courses, I felt his foot nudge mine. "Oh, I'm sorry…" I was startled and pulled back a little. His foot followed me and, to my mild irritation at myself, my cheeks reddened again. We continued to play footsie as we shared my lightly spiced salmon and his lamb tagine. It was something I'd not done since… inwardly smiling, I remembered it was Alex who'd introduced me to the delights of foot foreplay, always under a formal dining table when we were eating with others which made the whole thing even more erotically improper.

He grinned at me. "Isn't this place fabulous? I worked here for a short while ages ago but can't resist coming back, I absolutely love it. I'm so glad you like it, but the best is yet to come, I promise." Just how much better could it get, I wondered. I was soon to find out.

We'd nearly finished our mains, when two musicians and three singers from London's Royal Opera House set up and started to play and sing to us for well over an hour while we grazed on mascarpone and coffee cake, accompanied by the strongest coffee I'd ever tasted. It was an utterly magical experience. I was completely captivated as we sat and listened to the divas perform from Madame Butterfly, Porgy and Bess, Carmen, La Traviata and the Phantom of the Opera, ending with a couple of rousing Queen songs.

The combination of excellent food, subtle flirting, and the amazing music plus two glasses of wine after the beer had made me positively maudlin and I found myself blinking back tears when the musicians took their final bow.

Having travelled into town by train, he'd accepted my offer to drop him back to Slough with alacrity. "I like travelling by train but the Sunday service is a bit hit and miss, isn't it?" We strolled to the station arm in arm and sat close on the tube.

I was surprised and rather pleased when, on the drive back, he'd asked me in. "At least have a cup of tea with us. I know Gran would love to meet you." I'd felt that was very sweet but wondered what she'd think of me. Don't be so silly my little voice said but I continued to feel nervous.

My misgivings were unfounded. I was warmly welcomed by an attractive, petite, elderly lady who was clearly well in her eighties. Her skin was a slightly darker café-au-lait than her grandson, thinning silver hair was in a neat bun at the nape of her neck, her hands were beautifully manicured, nails a pale pink and she was wearing a very pretty flowery shirt-waister style dress. Unfortunately, she was a little hard of hearing which made chatting to her while Sam made us tea a tad challenging. She was obviously his greatest fan and showed me some family photos, mainly featuring him. "He's such a good boy. Always makes time to visit me. And he makes wonderful cakes, nearly as good as mine."

The three of us sat in her small sitting room cluttered with lots of family photographs and ornaments, drinking Lady Grey tea and eating minute cupcakes. "Gran doesn't eat much these days," Sam explained softly. "So, I make these for her. I get a real kick out of when she says they're good but not as good as hers."

Hers must have been spectacular because what I was eating was cake-heaven. He'd made honey and cinnamon, lemon drizzle, and a gooseberry fool – each one a tiny morsel of pure delight.

The afternoon flew by but I had work on Monday, so after another hour I said a reluctant goodbye to my hosts whereupon I was given hugs from both. Sam walked me to my car and we kissed – toe-curling, spine-tingling, breath-taking kisses – reminding me of when I was a teenager when all we did was grope a bit and kiss for so long, we end up with bruised lips... delicious memories. I drove away and was smiling for the whole journey home. And later as I thought about the conversations we'd had, I realised that very little had been said about Sam's past, apart from his grandmother's memories of his childhood, but that's to be expected from an older lady I thought so that made sense to me.

One evening Sam called and suggested we go for a picnic down by the river as it looked as though the weekend was going to stay warm and then talked about who would bring what – that gave me great pleasure. "I'll pick you up then, shall I?" That jolted me. I wasn't sure how I felt about him coming round to mine but it seemed churlish, not to say childish, to refuse.

We'd divided up who was going to bring what so after I'd prepped my contributions, I went to get myself ready. It was still wonderfully warm so I decided to wear a dress. As I sorted through my wardrobe, telling myself it was time for yet another clear-out, I noticed the lilac dress Richard had bought me – it was only a matter of a few months ago when it had been thrust into my hands but now felt like a lifetime. The skirt was wide enough for me to be able to sit on the grass in comfort if need be and the little jacket ideal for when it turned a little cooler. Downstairs again, I pulled out two folding chairs from the mess I called my pantry, which was in reality a pokey little cupboard under the stairs.

He was nothing if not punctual, this time in pale denims and a pale pink t-shirt with a darker pink sweatshirt tied carelessly round his shoulders which looked amazing against his dark skin. As I was ready, we loaded his car which was a rather nice white BMW convertible with red leather seats and a red roof. I did notice though that it was about ten years old and, for some reason, that made me feel more affection for him; clearly, he wasn't flashy. I'd never liked ostentatiousness, much preferring an understated good taste.

Yes, he would like a coffee he said in answer to my almost automatic question. We sat in the garden, he stroked the cat who'd seemed to have taken a liking to him, we talked, and I relaxed. More and more he seemed like a genuinely pleasant, amusing, agreeable man. I was looking forward to seeing his idea of a good picnic place.

I took the cups in and while I washed up, he went upstairs to the bathroom. I realised I wanted a wee too so sat on the top step, waiting for him to vacate, standing as soon as the door opened. I took a step towards the bathroom and was enfolded in a tight embrace.

I forgot all about wanting a wee. I was too busy being kissed and returning kisses. He stroked my cheek with one hand while the other rested just below my waist to keep me close.

I really hadn't planned on going to bed with him. And I couldn't even blame too much to drink – I was stone-cold sober. But, end up in bed we did. His healing passion swept over me, washing away any preoccupation about my body or being adversely judged. We kissed more and more feverishly as we clung together tightly before clumsily pulling at each other's clothes. I could hardly breathe – our kisses were so deep I felt was drowning. His tongue skimmed my lips and traced down to my breasts, tugging and nibbling at my nipples softly with his teeth and then moved down my stomach which instinctively I tried to keep as flat as possible. His mouth grazed my hips – I moaned in desire running the backs of my fingers down his sides and over his belly making him squirm.

I leaned over him to kiss and lick his chest, nipples and stomach before we locked together. I closed my eyes as I felt his hard insistence and, as our movements got faster and faster, couldn't stop my little squeaks and moans. He was a very skilful lover; it was as if he could read my mind and moved in ways that had me moaning in appreciation. Amazingly it almost felt like we'd been to bed together many times before. I didn't come but as I felt his jerking orgasm and his heart beating wildly next to mine, a warm feeling swept over me, not exactly a climax but almost better. As our breathing slowed, I snuggled into his shoulder. He turned and kissed my cheeks, my eyes, my chin my lips whilst one hand drifted down to explore and stroke me until I'd wriggled and gasped into intense spasms of pleasure.

"Oh... my... God..." was all I could whisper. He chuckled before kissing my mouth once more, this time gently biting my lower lip.

Neither of us was completed naked and while we readjusted ourselves, I noticed he had a couple of tattoos; one was a broken circle with small dragonflies escaping from it on his left shoulder, the other a Celtic-type pattern around his right bicep.

Tattoos weren't particularly my thing but was learning to love them, especially after Susie had sent me a picture of her most recent one a couple of months ago – two lines of small elegant Italian script on the side of her left foot – 'se domani non sei una persona migliore di quanto sei oggi, che bisogno hai per domini' which she'd translated as 'if you are not a better person tomorrow than you are today, what need have you for tomorrow'. I'd had to admit the tattoo itself was very pretty and certainly couldn't argue with the sentiments.

I traced the circle lightly with my fingertips. "A few years ago, I seemed to be going to funeral after funeral," he said, gazing out of the window introspectively. "Someone showed me this picture and it seemed the perfect one for me to live with it – I had to let go of some of the grief – I was drowning in it." My heart went out to him as I heard his pain and softly kissed the tattoo.

Whilst the skin on his body was deliciously smooth, his hands were a testament to outside work, they were slightly rough which I'd found strangely arousing, especially when he caressed my breasts. When I mentioned his injured middle finger, his brief answer of, "Comes from my druggie days," was in a tone that told me he didn't want to talk about it.

Just before leaving my bedroom, I picked up my bottle of Eternity eau-de-toilette to give myself a refreshing spritz. He laughed and when I asked why, explained one of his favourite colognes was Eternity for men. "Seems like we have very similar tastes… in many things," was his murmured comment as we made our way downstairs.

We still had our picnic – but in my garden. We unloaded the car and laid everything out on the grass. We ate tiny cucumber sandwiches and pieces of smoked salmon that we shared with Biba and Bon-Bon who'd insisted on joining us, crudités and sticks of assorted vegetables and a dish of humus he'd made. We drank Bucks Fizz. We nibbled on strawberries I'd macerated in balsamic vinegar before dipping them into melted white chocolate. We then dunked his home-made shortbread into steaming mugs of coffee. Throughout all this, baroque-style music played by Rondo Veneziano softly drifted into the afternoon. And as we ate and drank, we talked, we laughed, we giggled, we flirted.

When it got too cool to remain outside in comfort, we packed up the picnic and took it through to the kitchen, going back into the garden for a final tidy. Holding a chair apiece, we stood facing each other for a few seconds before I followed him into the warmth of the house. I put the chairs away and then made some fresh coffee.

"What's your favourite colour?" I paused while thinking of my answer. "To wear?" he added quickly.

That was easy. "Red. I like black and white too... but my absolute fave has to be red. Why?"

He ignored my question. "So, do you really like that dress?"

I blinked at the question. "It's a dress. It's ok. It's comfortable..." I didn't know what he was driving at.

He looked me up and down critically. "I'm not sure that I like it. I really don't think that colour does you justice. Why did you buy it?"

I looked down at the dress. He was quite right; the colour really wasn't me. I'd stopped to look at it because I quite liked the design but even at the time, knew I'd have preferred it in a different colour.

"Will you wear it again?" Another odd question.

"I... don't know. Maybe." I glanced down. "Actually, maybe not. Why do you ask?"

He sounded very firm. "Well, I don't think you should wear it again." He took a pair of kitchen scissors from the rack above the hob. "No... no, really you shouldn't..." It sounded like he'd made a decision.

He knelt in front me of, scissors in hand and made the tiniest of tiny cuts at the hem, between my calves. I gasped at his audacity but said nothing. He looked up and grinned before bending to his self-appointed task.

Of course, I could have stopped him – and heaven knows why, but I didn't. I stood stock still while, very slowly and very deliberately, he continued snipping at the dress – up the wide skirt and past my hips, waist, between my breasts before the final slice into the neckline. It now hung rather forlornly, like an open coat. Each impertinent, unhurried cut triggered yet another sharp intake of breath so that by now not only did the atmosphere between us positively crackle but I could barely breathe.

He pulled me to him, holding my face in both hands as we kissed slowly and gently, tongues skimming over teeth, lips softly bitten. We stood toe to toe, hip to hip, breast to chest, still kissing.

He reached down, grasped my bottom and lifted me so I ended up perched on the edge of the kitchen worktop. Standing between my legs he cut my knickers off me; I did have a momentary pang as the realisation that they were a new-ish pair of pretty black lace ones hit me but that was quickly swept away by the sheer sexiness of the moment. He nuzzled, licked and softly bit my nipples through the black material of my bra, it was like little bolts of electricity were sparking all over my body, I moaned softly as I felt myself want him more and more.

He pulled my hips into his and, staring into my eyes, thrust hard and fast. I clung to him mindlessly, feeling his hands holding my legs, his cock buried deep. Our excitement climbed higher and higher until, with a cry he came. He stood, panting and trembling slightly, clutching my legs as my final spasms abated and then stepped back. I pulled the dress round me and crossed my legs in a vain attempt to be ladylike. A bit late for that my little inner voice said and I giggled.

He stayed – of course he did. We drank the now-cool coffee with some Tia Maria I'd found lurking at the back of the dresser and then went to bed where we made gentle love again before drifting into sleep.

It was a truly fabulous day – and night...

Chapter 7

We got together quite a lot after that. It was only after several weeks when it dawned on me that we either went out which was always lovely or he came to Stratford and stayed at mine – both were shades of Richard which triggered slightly perturbing thoughts. And once I'd became aware, it increasingly bothered me. Every time I thought to raise the subject, I remembered that he had introduced me to his grandmother where I'd seen lots of photos of him and others, presumably family members. And he'd told me his only brother had died as a small child, that his parents had split up when he was eleven, that his mother had remarried, he didn't get on with his stepfather, and that he'd lost touch with his father. It was all perfectly plausible and certainly fitted in with the odd things his grandmother had mentioned.

Still, I found it disconcerting, so naturally I discussed it to my girlfriends. "You know what single men are like," Carrie had said. "Probably house shares or something like that."

"Maybe he's just in between houses," Anita suggested. Then why hadn't he mentioned it, I wondered.

"Maybe he's a serial axe murderer," giggled Chrissie. Her small boutique stocked the most unusual clothes – for the larger woman I'd been delighted to discover when it had first opened. I was always popping in the hope that there'd be something wonderful which was all too often the case, the elegant blue and cream striped one being a case in point. Her clothes weren't the only reason why people kept returning though – she had an elderly basset hound called Albert who, apart from coming to say hello to his favourite customers, happily snoozed his days away snuggled up in his basket which had been strategically placed to catch every possible sunbeam; I'd taken to sneaking him the odd sausage that, I was delighted to say, had made me one of his preferred visitors. Chrissie was an attractive, petite, bubbly woman who wore her long blonde hair in a high ponytail. She had the most one of the most romantic stories I'd ever heard. Some years before, she'd been working as a fund-raiser for a local charity who had recently hired an accountant. They worked together and got on very well. By coincidence one summer, they'd taken off the same three weeks, both returning to work saying they'd been feeling unwell – headachy and generally out of sorts. A couple of conversations later they'd realised they'd both been suffering from lovesickness – literally pining for each other. They married that September and been blissfully happy ever since. Chrissie had always dreamed of having her own shop so, with Alan's help and unstinting support, 'Chrissie's Closet' had opened and, almost immediately, started enjoying great success. It was tales like that that restored one's faith in happy-ever-after endings. When I'd first heard her story, it had made me think of Alex and almost given me fresh heart that I too might find my happy-ever-after ending – in fact it hadn't been long after that I'd signed up on the dating website. But in this case her contribution, I firmly told her, was not one little bit helpful.

"He's married. Definitely…" was Helena's opinion. Oh God, not another cheater I thought.

None of that helped much, apart from Carrie whose judgement of the situation was more or less mine.

I decided to ask him direct. "Actually, I've got this tiny attic flat in our Nottingham pub. One or two of the overseas staff live there too. It's okay, we all muck in and it's quite fun, but you'd hate it. And it's so much nicer at yours anyway. So, what's the problem, Lucie?"

Despite his breezy approach, I still felt there were a couple of problems. Primarily it reminded me all too vividly of Richard and his 'oasis of calm' remark used to justify keeping me at arm's length from the rest of his life, and the second was that it seemed very odd for a man of his age not to have his own place. But I supposed if he'd always been in hospitality and probably moved around a bit, then why not? And when he'd said, "I'd rather be cash rich than asset rich. Life's too short not to enjoy the finer things, don't you think?" I had to acknowledge there was sense in that and it reinforced that he must be single which had reassured and comforted me.

And it was so lovely to have someone who was so enthusiastic in bed with me and said, if not truly believed, I was beautiful. To have someone who liked the same music as me and was prepared to play bridge, albeit badly, just because he knew I liked it. To have someone who treated me like I was something very precious often arriving with flowers, wine, chocolates, even perfume once.

And maybe, just maybe, he was right. Maybe living for the moment, not putting down roots, having a more carefree existence was preferable to being mortgage and possession bound. Before Susie had made her unexpected entrance, Alex and I had occasionally talked about selling up, buying a boat and just taking off. It had all seemed like a silly pipedream at the time but Alex had once said, very seriously, that one of his major regrets was that we'd never even tried to do anything like that. 'What amazing memories we'd have created' was how he'd put it. I'd been too scared of the risks but could now see Alex's earnest and rather sad face in my mind's eye. Maybe he'd been right all along, it would have been a better way to live.

So, I continued to see Sam and enjoy his excellent company, not to mention his amazing imagination in bed. There was one night in particular. We'd stayed in, at mine of course, and cooked dinner together which was something I loved doing. I'd always felt co-cooking was one of the ultimate forms of foreplay and it became very clear he felt the same as we tasted from each other's spoons and fingers.

We'd eaten well but agreed to skip dessert and take a bottle of Prosecco to bed which he brought up in an ice bucket with a couple of glasses. He'd brought a DVD of an old movie, 9½ Weeks, with him so we lay in bed watching the film unfold.

He suddenly leaned away from me. "Close your eyes now." He sounded very authoritative. I obeyed.

"Open your arms." I did so, quivering in anticipation.

I heard a clinking sound, then gasped as I felt the chill of an ice-cube being run from my hairline, down my forehead, over my nose, across my open lips, down my chin and throat and between my breasts. "Stay still." I'd arched my back to meet his touch.

The slowly melting ice-cube was circled round my nipples, grazed down my stomach and left in my belly button. After a few moments I could feel water trickling across my waist and then his tongue lapping at it. I reached down to touch him only to have my hands gently slapped away. "I told you to open your arms." Silently I obeyed.

"Now, spread your legs." I took a sharp breath. I was now lying spread-eagled, eyes closed, not knowing what was going to happen next.

I screamed – he'd put an ice-cube in his mouth and was licking and softly nibbling my pussy. The cold of the melting ice and the warmth of his tongue was electric and I wriggled only to have the inside of my thigh softly bitten in reproof. I tried to remain still while his mouth returned to me until minutes later, I shuddered into release.

I sensed him move. "Stay as you are." I obeyed, heart pumping. I heard a crunching sound and then felt his fingers very gently pushing a piece of ice into me closely followed by his cock. It was the most incredible sensation. I couldn't stop myself – I threw my arms around him and this time wasn't scolded. More shudders overtook me and I clung to him, biting down on his shoulder as wave after wave shook me. I knew that he came but couldn't have said when. I was far too deeply immersed in my own pleasure.

After, I don't know how long, I opened my eyes, he was lying on his side next to me, watching me with a gentle smile. "Incredible." We both said it at the same time and our kisses were deeper and more impassioned than ever before. We slept entwined.

It was shortly after that memorable time he suggested we go away for the weekend. It wasn't that I didn't want to go but although work had been plentiful, actually getting paid from one of my clients was proving difficult so my bank balance had suffered. Coping financially – especially after both my fridge and washing machine had decided to give up their respective ghosts within a week of each other – had always bothered me. Despite the many advantages of being freelance, I often struggled with juggling cashflow – the main penalty of self-employment. Never mind, my overdraft would have to take the strain.

We arranged that I'd meet him at The Old Grey Mare, a pub on the banks of the River Avon close to the Pulteney Bridge in Bath, that was being turned into a gastro pub come bed-and-breakfast. "It needs a bit of work to bring it up to par, but the food's really good there and it's right by the river. I think you'll like it."

The drive down was very pleasant and my trusty sat-nav led me to the pub easily enough. I parked next to Sam's shiny white car that had the roof down and, for the umpteenth time, wished I had a convertible. The grey-stone building looked a little tired but the small gardens were beautifully tended. I could see Sam's hand in them.

He was standing at the bar, chatting to two members of staff. We took our drinks into the garden and sat under a leafy pergola and gazed at the river. The pub had its own little landing stage, a lovely romantic touch.

The outside of the pub might have needed some work but our bedroom was impressively decorated in shades of charcoal and cream dominated by a king-sized sleigh bed covered in silk cushions.

The one vibrant colour in the room were some bright red dahlias with sprigs of rosemary in a tall frosted glass vase. I looked at them in delight. They were beautiful. "I remember you wore red the first time I saw you and thought how absolutely stunning you were." His voice was soft. Wow, I thought, just wow.

"Let's go and eat – I know just where you'd like." We left the hotel and strolled into the city that boasted many fine Georgian buildings including of course, the beautiful Nash Terrace. We ended up in a small bistro, the Jars Meze, a family-run Greek restaurant. Their extensive menu led us to discussing the pros and cons of all the different dishes. Eventually we managed to agree we'd share a starter billed as 'Sharing is Best' which included courgette balls which tasted an awful lot better than the name suggested, spicily fragrant stuffed grape leaves, minty tomato fritters, fennel salami, a highly seasoned chicken liver pâté and some rustic bread to which we added cauliflower fritti, crispy shallot rings, olives, and crunchy kale slaw. We spent nearly an hour nibbling our way through the delicious morsels, washed down with most of a bottle of Robola, a wonderfully crisp, citrusy white wine hailing from sun-kissed Kefalonia.

Sam had decided on moussaka but, as the emptied plank was taken away, I asked if my pastitsio, a dish not unlike an Italian lasagne, be starter size. Both were delicious as I discovered when, yet again, we dipped into each other's dishes.

Having a whole dessert each was far too much but we both were captivated, so decided to share, the feta me meli, a slice of feta wrapped in filo pastry before being baked with Greek honey poured over the resultant pie – the balance between the salty feta and the sweet honey was delectable. We drank Greek coffee served in the traditional long-handled copper pots, accompanied by shards of bitter, black chocolate.

The streets became less crowded the closer we got to the pub. We stopped to kiss several times so by the time we were back in our room, we just couldn't wait and, pulling each other's clothes off, dived into the softness of the bed where we made tempestuous love.

After a truly delicious full English breakfast, we wandered outside and made our way to the centre of the city. American-style, we bought take-away coffees and continued to wander the streets, sipping as we went, eventually ending up at the Roman Baths where we spent over an hour at the Roman Temple, Roman Bath House and finally the Museum. As it was my first visit, I found everything fascinating, but as Sam had been several times he made an excellent guide, explaining much of the history as we made our way through the various parts of the buildings.

I found myself admiring his broad range of interests and expertise; I'd always been a sucker for bright, intelligent men.

You be careful, the little voice in my head warned me, you'll be falling in love with him next, won't you?

That was a bit late. I'd already fallen – I really had.

It started to rain and as we were close to an independent bookshop called Good Buy Books, we spent a very happy hour there. I bought Sam a book about Capability Brown and, because I'd loved reading Sherlock Holmes as a child, he bought me a Conan Doyle first edition.

Sam said he wanted to take me to a fantastic Moroccan restaurant, the Tagine Zhor, so we made our way there for about eight o'clock.

It was just like walking into North Africa. The walls were painted a dark terracotta, there were dusky shades on the lights giving an authentically ethnic ambiance and lots of flickering candles casting a warm glow on every table. There were lots of Moroccan pictures everywhere along with mirrors of different shapes and sizes that made the most of the soft lighting, and plush cushions were piled on the chairs. We were shown to a small secluded table and left to scan the huge menu. "I'm in your hands with this. I know so little about Moroccan food."

"I like the idea that you're in my hands." He stared at me for a moment before scanning the menu in earnest. "Shall we have another sharing starter?"

It was sublime – a selection of meats ranging from a Moroccan lamb sausage to spicy chicken wings and accompanying falafel and then a vegetarian's dream of hummus, mushrooms, aubergines, and other vegetables with a variety of spicy dips. It was all beautifully presented and absolutely delicious. In our enthusiasm to share, we ended up feeding each other which was erotic beyond belief and when, as we were finishing the last of the platter, I held his hand to lick baba ghanoush from his fingers it became abundantly clear the effect I was having on him.

We went on to share a lamb tagine along with a chicken and couscous dish incorporating shards of different vegetables with chickpeas and raisins covered with a pungently delicate sauce. We ate very slowly and drank slower still, talking all the time, while the waiters smiled indulgently at us. It was just as if we were kids in the first flush of love, unable to keep our hands off each other. We intertwined our fingers as we talked and occasionally dropped our hands to touch each other lightly under the table. We ate from each other's forks which was unbelievably intimate – I never wanted it to end.

We didn't leave until about one in the morning and, as it was drizzly, took a taxi back. On the drive, he ran his fingers lightly up and down my thigh until I was almost squirming. The minute we closed the door of our room behind us, he held me very, very close and then, teasingly slowly, undressed me as if I was a precious parcel, caressing the bits he exposed. He kissed my mouth, flicked his tongue over my ears, softly bit my throat, my breasts, my stomach and then, gently pushing my legs apart, nuzzled and licked me from one shuddering pinnacle of pleasure to another that took me even higher until I could take no more and begged him to stop.

The next morning, he suggested we breakfast somewhere else, so again we made our way into the city centre, then on to North Parade from where he led me down a narrow passageway to a small frontage with the sign 'Sally Lunn's House' over the door. We managed to find a small table by the window that had just been vacant and as we looked through the menu, Sam told me about the place. There'd been a young Huguenot refugee, Solange Luyon, who'd fled to England in 1680 to escape persecution. She'd somehow ended up in Bath and managed to find work in this very bakery, although, in those days, the street was known as Lilliput Alley. She began baking what she knew best, a rich, generous brioche bun, which astonishingly was the perfect accompaniment to both sweet and savoury toppings. Very quickly, this became a very popular delicacy in Georgian England, and soon customers were flocking to Lilliput Alley bakery, specifically requesting the Solange's amazing buns.

I sat listening to him, chin cupped in both hands, gazing fixedly at him. He suddenly stopped, looking self-conscious. "I don't mean to bore you…"

"You know I adore talking about food. Learning the history of a place like this is fascinating."

Because sweet toppings were reserved for the tops of the buns and savoury for the bottom, we opted for scrambled eggs and a cinnamon butter, accompanied by a refillable pot of coffee. The buns were absolutely huge and as we tackled first the savoury and then the sweet, we agreed the part bread/part cake was a match made in gastronomic heaven.

Afterwards we strolled a few calories off by heading towards Victoria Park to look at the Royal Terrace. I wasn't prepared for the sheer scale of the thirty Georgian terraced houses that were spread before me, the almost white stone gleamed in the sunshine. It looked familiar as many period dramas had been filmed there. We made our way to Number One which housed a museum, decorated and furnished in the style of the late seventeen hundreds which I found enthralling, much as I'd been captivated by the Wallace Collection near Marylebone the previous year.

"I know we don't want to eat just yet…" Sam started.

"We absolutely don't." I could still feel Sally's buns lying all too heavily.

"But we will later," he continued. "What do you fancy?"

I stopped to think for a moment. "What do I fancy? Well…" I stood still and looked at him. "Why don't we have a picnic?" Memories of our last picnic had just come flooding back.

He looked puzzled. "It's a bit chilly for that this evening, isn't it?"

"I wasn't thinking of picnicking in the park." I looked deep into his eyes and ran my fingers down his arm. "More of a picnic in slightly more…" I hesitated for a moment, "…horizontal comfort."

He blinked and raised a quizzical eyebrow. "Leave it to me." He pulled out his mobile and dialled, his eyes never leaving mine. When someone picked up, he turned away from me and spoke softly for a few moments. "All sorted." He turned back and kissed the end of my nose. "Let's go…" He took my hand.

We passed a traditional-looking pub, the Old Green Tree, and at his suggestion, stopped for a quick drink. He talked about the pleasure of waiting for treats. "I rather like deferred gratification," he explained over his beer. "Don't you think that waiting makes whatever you're waiting for even better?" Oh my God, I thought, it most certainly did.

The now-familiar bedroom opened before us. Luckily it was quite a large room because someone had set up a small folding table, two dining chairs, linen, glasses and cutlery and on top of the table was a very large box.

"Think I'll change for dinner," I murmured and went into the bathroom where I freshened my makeup, spritzed perfume into my hair and put on a spaghetti-strapped, wide-skirted black and white spotted maxi-dress, just to look a little different, hopefully invitingly flirty.

I opened the door to see Sam standing at the window, gazing across the still river. He heard me and turned. As I swished my way towards him, he smiled – appreciatively I hoped. Laying my hands very lightly on his shoulders, I kissed his cheek. I felt his hands on my waist and as he pulled me into him, took a small step back. "'Deferred gratification' I think you said?" He chuckled. I glanced down at the table. "Dinner not ready yet?" I tried to sound stern. "Tsk, tsk – what a bad boy."

He bowed his head. "I'm so sorry." He held a chair out for me. "Would you care to sit?"

I did so and watched as he busied himself putting the food out, making sure our places were laid correctly. "I'd like a drink now I think," I ordered after a few moments.

"Certainly madam." He threw a towel over his arm to play waiter, deftly opened a chilled bottle of prosecco and handed me a brimming glass.

"You may pour one for yourself." I'd never done so before but found taking a bossy role quite a turn-on.

He poured another glass and went to sit down. "Really?" I raised an eyebrow.

He stood close to me as I held up my glass and we solemnly clinked. We sipped and I put down my glass. As I did so, he bent and caught my hand, turning it to kiss the palm. I pretended to be unmoved and picked up my glass again. Holding his gaze, I took another sip and put my glass down again. "Closer please." I remained seated and, holding onto the front of his pale blue shirt, pulled him down to me. As his face drew close to mine, I stroked his cheek and then kissed him, skimming my tongue over his teeth before biting at his bottom lip. The moment I felt him respond, I pushed him away.

Slowly I picked up my glass. "I wonder..." I waited for all of ten seconds, "I wonder if we should fuck before dinner." I couldn't believe I'd just said that.

No-one could say he couldn't take a hint. He scooped my skirt up to my waist, bent me over the back of a chair and, seconds later was fucking me so hard and fast I had to brace my hands on the seat of the chair to keep my balance. Seconds after his convulsive orgasm he withdrew but as I started to straighten up, was pushed back down again as he stroked, rubbed and teased me into my own explosive release.

He pulled me up, wrapping his arms around me, his mouth to my ear. "Will there be anything else... madam?" Still trembling, I shook my head.

I hadn't realised that his jeans, rather tantalisingly, had a button fly and when he tucked himself back into his trousers, he'd left the top button undone. For some reason, I found the slightly agape waistband improperly erotic and took a deep breath at the thought of more pleasures to come.

He returned to the table, replenished our glasses and beckoned me to sit. As in the Tagine Zhor, we shared each delicious morsel, kissing and touching at every opportunity while chatting and giggling non-stop. Two hours sped by. Dipping into the last of the sharp lemon meringue cheesecake and gooey chocolate brownie that had been provided, Sam took my hands to slowly lick and suck each finger. "Messy girl... think I need to fix you..." He stood without a word and disappeared into the small ensuite leaving me sitting alone.

The sound of running water and a lovely hot soapy smell wafted into the room. A few moments later he reappeared, took my hand and gently pulled me towards him.

Leading me into the bathroom, he peeled my clothes away, then helped me into the foaming bath of bubbles. "I'll get us a little drink." Moments later he returned with refilled glasses and sat on the edge of the bath but didn't stay there for long.

It was the first time I'd made love in a bath – it was mind-blowing. We sat facing each other and as he slowly lowered me onto his straining cock, we kissed and slid our hands over each other's warm, soapy bodies. I could barely contain the incredible sensations washing over me and as we rocked, kissed, caressed and softly scratched, our excitement mounted until we cascaded into blissful ripples of pleasure.

We sat gazing at each other over the breakfast table. We'd arrived downstairs as late as we dared and lingered as long as possible. We sat in the garden with our second coffees, scanning the morning papers. I couldn't believe the days had flown by so quickly. The thought of leaving what had become our grey and white sanctuary made me sad.

However, our respective realities were calling, so we rose to our feet and, holding hands, made our way back to our beautiful room. We packed silently, then hugged. "It's been the most wonderful weekend. Thank you so much," I murmured into his neck.

"Such a pity it can't go on..." he started and then, holding each other's faces, we kissed gently before picking up our cases and, without a backward glance, left.

He saw me into my car and I drove away, seeing him waving and getting smaller and smaller and as I did, for some reason I really couldn't fathom, fat tears ran down my cheeks.

I'd only driven ten miles or so when I realised the petrol gauge was showing close to empty. Better get fuel before I hit the motorway, I thought so stopped at the next garage I saw. After filling up, I went to pay and, much to my irritation with myself, couldn't find my reading glasses. Fortunately, I managed to see just enough to be able to key in my pass numbers. Back in the car, I went through my handbag – no sign of them nor the case I usually kept them in. I sighed in impatience. There was nothing for it, I'd have to retrace my steps and just hope I'd left them in the room.

I noticed there was no white BMW when I pulled into the small carpark. It was lucky I'd returned, not only had I left my glasses in the bathroom, my mobile charger had fallen off the bedside cabinet and had been found under the bed. I thanked the barmaid warmly and accepted her offer of yet another coffee before setting off again. The view across the river was so nice, I had to sit outside. "Yes, Sam was urgently needed at our Gloucester place, otherwise he'd have stayed here to help us out for a few days; our manager's been off sick for a while so we're under quite a lot of pressure," was the answer to my query as to where Sam might be. I nodded understandingly and then sat in stunned surprise as she explained that Sam was one of two troubleshooting bar-tenders-cum-waiters, servicing the dozen or so pubs in the small chain. So, he was a member of staff – not part-owner as he'd said.

And it wasn't as if that mattered at all to me. What did matter a very great deal was that he'd lied. In pensive mood, I finished my coffee and left.

Sam called me that evening and after our initial hellos and how-are-yous, I took a deep breath and broached the subject that had been bothering me since I'd left the Mare. There were a few seconds of silence before he spoke. The upshot was very simple – he'd felt like I was out of his league, that I wouldn't consider seeing a 'mere' bartender, that he'd fancied me the minute he'd seen me, and once the... exaggeration was what he called his lie, had been said, he felt he had no way of going back on it.

I didn't know whether to be disappointed, flattered or angry – it was probably a combination of all three. "You really think I'm that shallow?" was my first question followed by "How long did you think you'd be able to keep this up?" and finally, "Don't you see, now you've lied to me, how can I trust whatever else you say to me?' I was almost in tears of frustration as he kept saying the same thing over and over again.

Eventually the conversation ended. I'd said what I felt needed to be said. In answer to his "Can't we see each other again? I really want to…" I'd half-heartedly agreed but not agreed as to where and when. The whole thing was left unsatisfactorily ajar…

Chapter 8

O ne of my go-to strategies whenever I was upset or needed to think things through was to attack a room for a proper tidy-up and declutter. This time was no exception. It had been ages since I'd sorted through my shoes and handbags so a very enjoyable hour or so was spent in deciding what should stay and what should go. As usual the pile of 'should go' things were much smaller than anticipated but nevertheless, I'd achieved something and felt heaps better.

Absent-mindedly I opened my underwear drawer to see the normal tangled mess and as I was in full reorganising mode, tipped everything on the bed. There was a load of saggy knickers along with sad-looking bras so they went straight into the rubbish bin. As I was folding what little was left and putting them back, it occurred how pitifully short of decent undies I was. The pair of black lacy knickers that had been so unceremoniously cut off me had been one of my few nicer pieces but I consoled myself their sacrifice had been worth it.

Anita called me that evening and suggested we get together so we arranged to meet for an early lunch at a café in the middle of town that Saturday. Time enough to sort through my boots I thought, and added a few more discards to the black sack that was now full enough to make a reasonable contribution.

On Saturday morning, I dropped the sack to the local hospice's charity shop. I'd decided to get into town early as I wanted to go to Marks & Spencer for some undie-replacements. After ten minutes of wandering round the racks, I picked up half-a-dozen pretty bras to try on. The first couple didn't fit as well so I picked up the third. I thought it would to be a bit tight and I was right. I peeled it off and crossly stared at myself in the mirror, thinking to ask the assistant for the next size. I reached for the buzzer, then stopped and looked at myself again. No, I hadn't been mistaken – just to the right of my left nipple, the skin didn't look quite as smooth as usual, there was a definite dimple I was fairly sure hadn't been there before. I watched myself reach up to touch it – the skin didn't feel exactly the same as normal, very slightly coarse, perhaps even a tiny bit bumpy. I checked my other breast and knew there was a discernible difference between the two. I sank on the stool, still staring at myself. I don't know how long I sat there but was suddenly aware of a tap on the door and an anxious voice asking if I was alright.

"I'm fine, thank you." I wasn't – I was hot, shaky, and felt I was going to throw up at any minute. I needed to get out. Ignoring the other bras, I hastily pulled on my clothes and opened the door.

"I'm so sorry, I'll be back later…" I left as quickly as I could.

I knew it would be too hard to have lunch and act normally with Anita so texted her, saying I had a really bad headache and could we make it another day? Her reply came almost instantly – of course she understood and looked forward to catching up very soon. 'Anything I can do?' Probably no, not right now, I thought as I said a grateful thank you but no thank you.

The minute I got home, I made myself a cup of very strong coffee and tried to rationalise what I'd seen, or thought I'd seen.

I felt sure my panic was in large part because I'd watched my mother battle breast cancer for the last few years of her life. She'd endured a mastectomy, chemotherapy and radiotherapy back in the days when the treatment was almost more savage than the disease. All her determination and fighting hadn't helped – she died in her mid-fifties, about six years after initial diagnosis. When I'd reached the age when she'd died, I was inconsolable, vowing to make the very best of the years left to me that had been so cruelly denied her. Maybe that was why Richard's behaviour – and Sam's come to think of it – were so hurtful; they were a sign of wasted precious time.

I'd almost convinced myself I was being silly when I thought to google breast cancer and seconds later was scrolling through articles and pictures. I froze. There was a photograph of a breast that looked just like mine – the tiniest patch of barely puckered skin that, after investigation, had proved to be stage three cancer. I swallowed hard, almost sure of the road I was about to travel.

My first instinct was to talk to Susie but, I reasoned, there was absolutely no point whatsoever in worrying her, especially as she was so far away and what could she do anyway? I thought of Anita, of Shona, of Carrie, of my other dear friends, but again it seemed ridiculous to burden them with what I hoped would be nothing. I'll tell them if and when there's something to say, I resolved.

I was so tempted to ignore the whole thing but after I'd gone into the bathroom with a torch to shine a bright beam on my breast and examined it very carefully, knew I couldn't just pretend it wasn't there. I was very lucky to get an appointment with a locum for the next afternoon – my own doctor was fully booked for over a week which was far too long to be reassured that my imagination might be in overdrive.

The locum was very thorough in her examination. After pulling my top back on, I tried to read her face. She looked up and smiled reassuringly before returning to the screen to make notes. "Well, there's a definite pucker I don't like the look of so I think it's best I book you in for a biopsy as soon as possible." She was taking it seriously; I took a shaky breath. "It's probably nothing to worry yourself about but it's wise to check these things out, don't you think?" She looked at me again.

"Oh yes. Absolutely. Always best to be sure." I knew I sounded calm but could feel heat rising as my stomach knotted painfully.

"You okay?" It felt like a perfunctory question.

"Yes. I just get a bit hot sometimes… it's my age." I laughed tremulously.

She smiled back at me saying I'd hear direct from the hospital about a date for my biopsy. "It's important you just relax as much as you can." I returned her smile much more calmly than I felt and left.

I'd received a couple of texts from Sam while waiting for an appointment letter from the hospital. I knew I must have been a bit offhand because his response to my second one was 'Look, if you don't want to see me, just say so.' That drew me up short. I hadn't meant to be unkind; it was just that I was so focused on what was happening, and what might very well happen. He deserved some kind of explanation so I called one evening. Unfortunately, I went to voicemail and as I couldn't think what to say, so just hung up. Half an hour later I called again and this time left a message where I apologised for being curt and said I wasn't very well but would be in touch soon.

The next day he called and of course asked what was wrong. I think it was when I burst into tears, he realised something was really amiss. He was very sweet, saying that if there was anything he could do he would, that he really wanted us to stay in touch, that I was to let him know what was happening, and of course he'd love to see me again no matter what was wrong. It was that last comment when I lost it and just couldn't speak for hiccupping sobs.

"You really must keep absolutely still Lucie – I'll try not to be too much longer." The examination couch was very hard and uncomfortable, it felt like I'd been lying on it for hours. Although the young radiographer's voice was soft and gentle, I knew she meant business so obeyed, but flinched involuntarily as I felt a sharp scratchy prick, very close to my nipple, to anesthetise the area prior to the actual breast aspiration. I closed my eyes as moments later, there was a steady, insistent pressure which was a larger needle being pushed deep into my breast to gather some cells for analysis; the scan I'd had a few moments before had shown unmistakeable abnormalities in the breast tissue. "At least we know exactly where we're heading," she'd said – she sounded positively cheerful

"Hmmm…" I opened my eyes at the second "Hmmm," noticing a small frown wrinkling her otherwise perfect brow. "Don't worry Lucie. It's…" She stared at the grainy image on the small screen by my head. The pressure on my breast stopped as she straightened up. "I'm just going to see Dr Forbes. Won't be a moment. You relax." I didn't have time to relax as seconds later she returned with a dark haired, harassed-looking man who gave me a kind smile.

"Gemma was having a bit of bother getting in," he said cheerfully as he pulled on latex gloves. He made it sound like we'd been unsuccessful in crashing into a rather exclusive party. The prolonged, oddly painful pressure on my breast returned for what seemed like many minutes but must have been much less. "There we are Gemma." He smiled triumphantly and the pressure eased as the needle was slowly withdrawn. He looked down at me. "All done. We'll see you next week to discuss the results. Okay?" And, with a reassuring pat on the shoulder, he was gone.

Gemma gently wiped the gel off my breast, put on a small plaster to cover the little puncture marks where the needles had gone in and held my hand as I sat up, albeit a bit unsteadily. "I'll leave you to get dressed." She gave me a slip of paper. "Take this to reception, they'll make an appointment for next week. No need to rush." The gel had left my skin a bit sticky so I didn't bother with struggling to get my bra on. I reapplied lipstick to make myself feel a little better before returning to reception to make my next appointment.

I stared at the consultant, unsure whether to laugh or cry.

"It's really good we found it at such an early stage," she'd said, smiling benevolently. "The mass appears to be pre-cancerous but our feeling is that with your history, it'd be better to have surgery sooner rather than later to remove it." She leaned forward as she saw my face. "It's just a day job Lucie. You'd be in for a few hours and then, depending on the results, that'll probably be the end of it."

Probably, she said 'probably' I thought, and nodded my agreement.

A few minutes later I was standing outside, clutching a form which I was told to bring with me for a pre-operation health check to be scheduled shortly. After I'd explained I worked on a freelance basis so it was trickier for me to take time out than if I'd had a 'proper' job, she'd assured me I'd hear about dates in the next few days and, that as it was a minor operation, all would probably be done and dusted within a couple of weeks. I'd resolved not to mention anything to my clients as I'd probably be back to normal working very soon. A few too many probablies for my liking but, given the consultant's upbeat comments, I felt relatively lucky about this.

I'd decided to use the word 'inconvenience' rather than anything more emotive.

The consultant was absolutely right. Ten days later I went for my pre-op check. Blood pressure was up a bit, but that was hardly surprising, the nurse told me. Pity I hadn't kept to my diet, she added, after I'd told her I'd been meaning to try and lose weight for a while. She's a fine one to talk I thought as I eyed the pale blue uniform straining over her hips but agreed a few pounds lost before the operation would be much better than not.

I was as good as my word. By the time I'd been summoned, I'd shed eight pounds – not that it had been hard work, I'd simply stopped eating bread and had completely lost the taste for alcohol. Both had made me feel much better. I'd also started to tell a few more close friends about my operation. Anita and her lovely husband Jeff had insisted I stay with them for at least one night afterwards, an offer I'd gratefully accepted, the thought of staying with them was so reassuring. Anita dropped me off, saying that as soon as she received a text from me, she'd be on her way to pick me up.

I waved her goodbye and made my way to the day-operation ward where I undressed, donned one of those deeply unflattering hospital gowns that did up at the back – thank goodness I was allowed to keep my own knickers on I thought – and waited. I was third on the list so didn't have too long to wait which I was very grateful for.

It must have been about lunchtime when I heard a caring voice. "Wake up Lucie. It's all over. Time to wake up…"

Opening my eyes seemed a huge effort but I managed it. There was a pretty young nurse standing by me. "Well done, Lucie. You take a few minutes. I'll be back in a moment." I blinked and looked down. There was a cannula in my left hand and I flexed my fingers irritably – I'd always hated needles, this one felt painfully alien. Ten minutes later I was feeling much better, still sleepy but better. I'd been allowed a few sips of water with the promise of a cup of tea later. "We need to make sure you're completely awake and feel ok before we let you go." Keen as I was to leave, that made sense.

A couple of days later, Shona and James returned from another of their holidays. Shona came over for coffee the next day. She looked bronzed and fit and obviously had had a lovely time. I told her what had been happening and she frowned. "You sure it's all okay?"

"I think so." I shrugged. "Of course they'll do some tests on what was taken away but all the signs were that it was pre-cancerous. So that's that." I knew I was sounding more confident than I felt.

Shona was still frowning. "Well, I certainly hope so but it might not be, you know. Just be prepared that you might need a bit more treatment."

"Always best to be optimistic," I said firmly and quickly changed the subject. "Tell me all about your holiday…"

Their mini-cruise round the Greek Islands sounded wonderful and I enjoyed hearing all about their visits to Delos, Mycenae, the Arkadi Museum, the White Tower of Thessaloniki and many more iconic places – they were real culture vultures and loved cruising so this holiday had been perfect for them.

The next morning Shona rang. "I meant to say yesterday – we recently joined this new health spa just out of town. It's really lovely. Why don't you join me one day? We can swim a bit, relax by the pool, have a spot of lunch… What about it?" What a great idea, I thought, so happily agreed she'd pick me up the following day.

It certainly was a beautifully appointed spa. There was a compact gym, a large pool with a small jacuzzi to the side and several very comfortable loungers draped with thick snowy white towels. It had been ages since I'd swum and I was really looking forward to it.

To my delight, the changing cubicles were slightly larger than average as were the lockers. "This is so civilised," I called over the partition to Shona and heard her laugh in amused pleasure at mine. I'd stripped off, started pulling my costume up and was just adjusting the top when I froze. I touched myself again to double-check. No, I was right. There was a lump – very small but nonetheless clearly detectible. It was high in my left breast, about two inches above the previous surgical site. And this time I knew – absolutely, heart-stoppingly knew – this time there was no doubt in my mind, it was cancer.

I leaned my forehead against the cool wall of the cubicle for a few moments but my legs were trembling so much I had to perch on the tiny bench. I bit down on my hand in an effort to regain a semblance of control.

Shona's door opened and closed, I heard the sound of a locker opening and closing. "Come on slowcoach." She paused. "You alright?"

I swallowed hard, feeling a sour taste of bile rising in my throat and mouth. "Yes. I'm fine. Be with you in a minute. You go on." I heard her bare feet pad away.

Taking a couple of deep breaths, I straightened up, readjusted my costume, gathered up my belongings, put them in a locker and made my way to the pool where Shona executing a very creditable crawl. Making myself smile, I joined her in the refreshingly cool water where we companionably swam a few lengths side by side.

The loungers were every bit as comfortable as they looked. We settled ourselves down and I pulled one of the fluffy towels over myself while Shona ordered some coffee. "Isn't this nice?" She smiled at me.

To my horror I felt tears on my cheeks. "What on earth…" She leaned over and held my hand. "Lucie, what is it?"

I shook my head in an effort to stop the tears. "Nothing. I'm okay."

"Don't be so ridiculous. I can see you're not. Tell me…"

I did. She sat in silence for a few moments before squeezing my hand, then stood and walked towards the changing room. She returned seconds later holding her mobile which she held out to me. "Ring your doctor and get an appointment. Now – right now. This minute."

There was no arguing with her. I made the call and was given an emergency appointment for half past eight the following morning. She frowned as I repeated the time. "Why not this afternoon?"

"Sho, there's no difference between this afternoon and first thing tomorrow morning."

"I suppose not." I could tell she didn't agree.

I insisted we spend the day as we'd planned. In fact, it felt so much better to have shared the shock of my discovery with someone I'd known and trusted for so long that I started to relax, properly relax, and actually enjoyed the rest of the day. We swam some more. We had a lovely lunch of slow cooked beef casserole with crusty bread. We went for a stroll in the hotel's rambling grounds. It was only when we sat in the vast lounge, sipping steamy hot chocolate, when we talked about my discovery again, by which time I was feeling very much calmer.

It was late afternoon when Shona dropped me home. We hugged affectionately as we said our goodbyes. Half an hour later the phone rang – it was Shona who told me again what she thought I should say to the doctor. She'd always had a keen interest in all matters medical, probably because her mother had been a doctor and when James had suffered a minor heart attack some years ago, she'd been an informed tower of strength, taking complete charge of his medication. I knew she only had my best interests at heart but gently stopped her in mid-sentence, telling her not to worry and assuring her I'd call her straight after my appointment. Bless her, I thought as I put the phone down.

Surprisingly, I slept very well and awoke refreshed. At eight thirty prompt I was lying on my GP's examination couch while he gently prodded my left breast. I tried to read his face as he did so. Afterwards, while I pulled on my baggy sweatshirt, he washed his hands and sat down. "You're absolutely right – there's definitely a small mass there. You need to be seen as soon as possible." He picked up the phone. Five minutes later he confirmed that I was to return to the hospital's clinic in three days. "Just be aware they might want to do another biopsy that day," he added. I nodded silently. By ten past nine I was sitting in a small waiting room at Stratford hospital, clutching a slip of paper, waiting for a blood test.

As the smiling nurse tightened the plastic strap round my upper arm, she looked at me. "Are you okay with this?"

I smiled back. "Well, I have to say I'd much rather not be sitting here but yes, I'm okay." I kept my eyes firmly fixed on a notice stating, rather unnecessarily in my opinion, the importance of hand-washing, as she tapped the crease of my elbow to encourage blood vessels to appear. "Think I've got shy veins." I was trying to start a distracting conversation.

She glanced up. "Most people don't like blood tests."

"I'm not surprised." I wasn't.

Much to my surprise, she giggled. I took a deep breath as the needle slid in. "There was this chap a week or so back. I asked him the same question – we always do just in case someone has a real issue. But he stared, really stared at me, and said that he really, really liked them." I gasped in astonishment and gazed at her; she was watching my blood seep into a second tiny tube. "Won't be long. I need three of them." She was concentrating hard.

Seconds later the third tube had been filled, the needle withdrawn, a small pad placed over the tiny hole and my forearm pushed up to hold it in place. "Anyway..." she continued as she jotted down my details on each tube, "...after I'd finished, as he pulled down his sleeve, he stared at me again and said 'that was so, SO good, thank you very much' and left. I just sat with my mouth open. No-one's ever said anything like that to me before." She giggled again. Well, well, I thought as I pulled on my jacket and left – it certainly takes all sorts.

When I rang Shona to give her an update, I recounted the story the phlebotomist had told me and happily found it made me laugh again, dissipating much of my tension. "I'm fine. Honestly. I know it might sound a bit odd, but all's cool – at least for the moment."

I remained upbeat for the next couple of days.

The consultant agreed with my doctor. There was definitely a tumour she said. That shook me – it was the first time that word had been used and somehow made things much more real. It was a very brief conversation. I was to return bright and early on Monday the following week for another biopsy but had to stay in overnight as she wanted to also remove one lymph node for analysis. "Just to make sure everything's staying local," she said as I took a breath to ask why that was necessary. My blood test hadn't shown anything untoward which was excellent news, she added.

Monday came round all too quickly. Again, Anita drove me, saying she'd take me to their's again when she picked me up the following day. Later, I was wheeled into an operating theatre and woke later feeling slightly more battered that before. Lifting my left arm was painful but I was assured that would diminish over the next few days.

This time, my recovery wasn't quite so smooth. The wound in my armpit required a small drain so a district nurse called each day until it was removed. I stayed with Anita and Jeff for the rest of the week, metaphorically licking my wounds and wondering what the tests would reveal. Much as I tried to remain upbeat, I had many dark moments when memories of my mother's struggle with her cancer surfaced and made me cry frightened, bitter tears.

The following Monday dawned dull and drizzly. I drove what was becoming an all-too-familiar route and sat in the waiting room with other cancer patients. It was very sobering.

My results were mixed. Apparently, the lymph was clear which meant everything was almost certainly contained within the breast. Another 'almost' I thought as the consultant smiled at me as if I was a bright student who'd just passed a particularly hard test. "However..." My heart sank. As a teacher, I'd always started with the positive and then say 'however' as a precursor to something negative before ending the conversation on as upbeat a note as possible. And I was right – it wasn't great news. The biopsy on the lump showed stage two cancer. This meant it was potentially possible other areas of the breast might well be 'cooking' further tumours. I smiled involuntarily – it seemed an odd way to describe something so deadly in such a mundane way.

I was moved on to discuss options with a softly-spoken cancer nurse who introduced herself as Zainab. She explained she acted as the link between consultant and patient. "I have more time to talk about details and give the pros and cons of the different steps you need to consider. So, Lucie, we have about half an hour to look at what can happen next. Let me get you a drink first." At that point I'd have quite liked a large gin and tonic but contented myself with a small cup of overly-strong tea.

Zainab explained the various options very clearly but more than once I found I had to ask her to repeat herself as my concentration drifted away. "Lots of people find it hard to take everything in at first," she said. That didn't reassure me much as I was used to being sharp and focused, especially when it came to my work. I delved in my handbag to find a notepad but couldn't find a pen so Zainab passed me hers. Just having a pen in my hand helped me gain a semblance of self-control and I started to breathe more easily.

Evidently the histology test had shown that in all probability a large enough margin for safety hadn't been taken in my previous operation, despite the surgeon's best endeavours. We went on to look at what else could happen. It boiled down to either a further lumpectomy which was not their preferred course of action or a full mastectomy which was. I leaned back in my chair, trying to take everything in. "If you do have a mastectomy, we can offer you reconstruction of course," Zainab added. We talked more as she explained that reconstruction meant more invasive surgery, a longer recovery time which would inevitably lead to a longer period of time unable to work. I took a deep breath and asked if I could opt to have reconstruction at a later stage. "Yes, of course," was the answer. I took a deep breath of relief. I knew I couldn't afford to be out of action for too long. "We really do feel that a mastectomy is the better option. That'll assure us, as far as is possible, that everything's been surgically removed." I asked when I needed to come to a decision. "As soon as possible really. We certainly don't want to give the cancer too long, do we?"

Now, that really did jolt me. It was the first time anyone had used the 'c' word and hearing it brought everything into incredibly sharp focus. Zainab knew what I was feeling and smiled compassionately. "It's an awful lot to take in, isn't it?" I nodded dumbly. "I think we ought to make another appointment for next week and discuss your decision then, don't you?"

I cleared my throat. "Yes. Thank you, Zainab." I returned her pen, made my slightly unsteady way to reception, waited for what seemed like ages to make my appointment and left.

Once home, I called Anita who let me ramble on about the unenviable options I was facing. Over the next few days, I saw as many friends as possible. Now, my cancer was talked about interminably. I thought it interesting most people referred to my 'mass', 'lump' or 'tumour' so, in an effort to make myself fully internalise what was happening to me, I deliberately, and perhaps in childish defiance, used the words 'my cancer' whenever talking about it – I found it kind of made things personal, making me feel an almost weird affection towards it.

Most people's opinion was to go for a mastectomy and have reconstruction at the same time so everything was done and dusted at the same time. After all, who wanted to have to hoick a fake boob into one's bra every day, someone said as they wrinkled their nose at the thought. It was that that I found the most upsetting – the realisation of losing a breast, being lopsided, how I was going to look in certain clothes, being seen as less feminine – all that cut awfully deep.

What if there was more cancer I thought, what if an implant masked something in future, what would happen when my right breast drooped even more as it was bound to with advancing years – then I'd have one perky and one saggy? And just how much longer would recovery be? The more I thought about it, the more I was convinced I should wait for reconstruction and once I'd made the decision, I felt so much better and started to sleep soundly, not suffering from the nightmares that had previously beset me.

'Can't wait any longer, really want to see you. Be at yours Monday about 3. See you then. Sam xx'

I read and reread his text. I'd managed to keep him at arm's length for quite some time which had given me much needed breathing space, even though I was a bit uncomfortable about my lack of openness.

'That'll be lovely. Looking forward to seeing you. L xx' As I pressed the send button, I smiled in recognition that his text had made me warm, wanted and cherished but despite his beguiling protestations, waves of nervousness about seeing him stayed with me for a long time.

On Monday morning, I made a dark chocolate mousse topped with curls of white chocolate and prepped some potatoes dauphinoise to accompany steak with a green salad and caper dressing. Dinner sorted, I showered and dressed with care. I'd chosen a dark blue lacy bra but immediately realised how much it irritated the skin on my left breast so reluctantly changed into an older, softer, tee-shirt bra.

Sam arrived laden with an armful of creamy-white lilies, and a bottle of prosecco. The minute he'd put the flowers and bottles down in the kitchen, I was engulfed in a warm hug. "God, I've missed you." His voice was muffled by my hair.

I hugged him back and then gently disentangled myself. "Drink?" My hand hovered over the kettle. He raised his eyebrows. "Shall we start off with a cuppa?" I was still off the alcohol.

I arranged the flowers in two vases as there were far too many for one, made tea, put some biscuits on a plate and took everything through to the sitting room where Sam had made himself comfortable. He took his tea and looked up. "Everything okay? You seem… different somehow."

I sat next to him and held his hand. "Sam, there's something I need to tell you. Something I probably should have told you sooner but had to get my head round before I did…"

Ten minutes later I stopped. He stared at me. "You mean you've been dealing with this all on your own? Lucie, you should have told me. I want to be there for you – you should know that. How would you feel if I was facing something like this and hadn't told you?" He seemed genuinely cross with me.

"I know Sam, I know. But I had the girls. And honestly, it's not as though we know each other that well, I didn't know how you'd feel, and anyway I kept thinking it'd be nothing so why worry you…" My voice tailed off. I knew he was right – I'd have probably felt upset had he not told me.

His arm was around my shoulders. With his other hand, he held my chin, very gently pulled me to him and kissed my cheek, my chin, my forehead and finally my mouth. They were tender, loving kisses that melted my heart. I didn't mean to, but leant against him and cried in relief that at last I'd told him and that he was proving to be so understanding.

He held my face in both hands as our kisses slowly became more and more passionate. Ever since I'd started on this rollercoaster, sex had been the very last thing on my mind but his lust, albeit mellow, slowly ignited my own longing. It was like we'd never stop kissing; I could hardly breathe. Eventually we broke apart, panting, and looked at each other. I raised both hands to the top button of my dark pink overshirt and slowly unbuttoned it. He watched what I was doing before gazing deep into my eyes. "You okay to…?"

"I'm very okay to…" I'd pulled my shirt off by this time and shrugged out of my little white vest top but instinctively left my bra on. He ran his hands over my shoulders and down my arms, kissing my throat as I threw my head back. Unhurriedly, he ran his hands down my back, gently kneading and pinching my skin, then returned up my sides to hold my face to his as we continued kissing. He leaned back, pulled off his sweater and undid the buttons of his sage-green and white striped shirt. I reached down, flipped open his belt buckle and slowly, very slowly, unbuttoned him. He fumbled at my jeans waistband until I pushed his hand away, undid them myself and pulled them off.

I'd almost forgotten how good he felt and gasped in pleasure as we started to fuck. I wrapped my legs around his hips and licked his ears. We rolled off the sofa onto the floor, still locked together and, clinging tightly to each other, rocked and bounced towards orgasm. Within a couple of minutes, he'd come – it had been a long time since we'd been close. I kissed away his laughing apologies as we pulled some of our clothes back on. I knew it would be my turn soon…

I cooked us an early dinner after we'd polished off the bottle of prosecco. Cobra beer apart, it was the first time I'd had a drink for some time so it took very little for me to feel a bit squiffy which he found very funny.

"And what about what's happening right now?" He sounded curious.

What indeed I thought. "It's a bit scary but lots of people have gone down this road and been okay, so I guess I'm holding onto that. And there're so many people around to give advice and support, I don't feel alone." I looked at him and it hit me I'd probably said the wrong thing – again. "And it feels so much better now I've told you. I'm sorry I left it so long but I really didn't want to burden you when you were so far away. And honestly, I thought it'd be nothing to worry about." Staring into his eyes, I held his hands, willing him to see things from my point of view.

Delighted though I'd been to see him, I was starting to feel tired. The last few weeks had been such a helter-skelter of emotions; the sanctuary of my bed had been appealing earlier and earlier. "Let's go to bed." I'd meant to sleep but it soon became clear sleep was what Sam had in mind.

Since my first visit to the hospital, I'd taken to wearing oversize tee-shirts in bed, finding them soft and comfortable. Unthinkingly I reached under my pillow for the one I'd worn the previous night and pulled it over my head. I heard Sam chuckle. "This what you wear when I'm not around?"

I looked over my shoulder. He was looking amused so I stuck my tongue out at him. "Yup. I don't wear lace and satin every night, you know."

He grinned and reached for me. "You're bloody sexy whatever you wear. Now, put your tongue away – just for the moment mind… and come here…" I obeyed.

"Arms up." He peeled the tee-shirt off and softly bit my neck. "Face down." I did as I was told, but in order to lie flat, tucked my arms under me to take any pressure off my left breast. I felt his hands brush down my sides, my hips and outer thighs before sweeping back up to be closely followed by his mouth, kissing and softly nipping my skin. It was heavenly, I moaned appreciatively to tell him he was doing absolutely the right thing and please not to stop. He continued to give the most wonderful shoulder, back and bottom massage that had me sighing and twisting under his hands. "Turn over." As I did, I saw his eyes flick towards my left breast before hastily looking away. My arousal vanished in a heartbeat and, for the first time with him, I deliberately faked it so he'd come quickly. He kissed my throat and shoulders before flipping me over again so that I was on all fours. I moaned, yelped and wriggled so convincingly that he came within moments and collapsed over my back.

The next morning, he was very sweet and loving. So much so, I wondered if it had been my imagination about what had unsettled me last night. Whilst I'd told him what was happening, I'd not gone into any detail about the decision facing me and felt now it was time to share. So, after one of my favourite breakfasts of crispy bacon and tomato-y scrambled eggs, I cleared the kitchen while he brewed some fresh coffee.

I cleared my throat. "I have to make a pretty a big decision very soon and I'd like to talk to you about it. It's about my cancer…" He visibly flinched. "Look, it's just there are options and it'd help me so much to talk it through with you…" I went on to say there was no question about needing further surgery, and sooner than later, but had to choose between a lumpectomy or mastectomy. "I've been offered reconstruction if I go for a mastectomy but, quite frankly, it's the recuperative time from such a big operation that's putting me off. And it's in my head that immediate reconstruction might well cover something up. You know – mask more cancer?" I stopped and looked at him. "What do you think?"

He took a deep breath. "What does the consultant suggest?"

"She thinks a mastectomy's the better option. She says she'd like to make as sure as possible that everything's gone." As the words left my mouth, I'd made my unequivocal decision.

"Well…" He sounded thoughtful. I held my breath, hoping his opinion would be in line with my thinking. "Well, if having the whole breast removed is the safer option, I think you should probably do that." I breathed again. "But I think you should go for reconstruction. I mean, why not have everything done at the same time?" I had to concede he had a point. "I mean, you'll have to take time out anyway. I can't see why it'd take that much longer to recover from having reconstruction than not. And wouldn't you rather have two breasts than one?" His voice was very slightly quavery and I suddenly realised my having only one breast was likely to bother him significantly more than me.

I smiled at him. "Thank you Sam. That's really helped. A lot. Bless you." I kissed his cheek.

"Listen Lucie. I can see there's an argument against reconstruction so if that's what you decide, of course I'll be there for you." He paused. "But I still think that's by far the better option. You asked for my opinion and that's it."

It was time to change the subject. I asked about the pub gardens he'd been planting up and as he talked about what he'd been doing, I felt relieved he'd been so easily distracted.

We went on to have a really lovely day. We strolled into town, walked by the river and watched an enthusiastic puppy have a stand-off with an adolescent but nonetheless fairly large swan. Much to our and the puppy's owner's amusement the swan won but as they walked away the puppy continued to yap defiance over his shoulder until he was firmly shushed. We enjoyed a drink on the terrace of the Dirty Duck and gazed through the bare branches of the waterside trees at a couple of barges making their slow way towards the marina. We mooched around town and gazed in a few shop windows at the new season's clothes on display. Inevitably we ended up at my favourite place where we shared a board of breaded brie with chilli jam, some whitebait with garlic mayo, crispy squid with lemon mayo and a dish of piquant tomato hummus with flatbread. All were scrumptious and we certainly couldn't manage much more but the salted caramel sundae and raspberry ripple cheesecake were far too tempting to ignore so we sampled both.

"So, what can I do to help?" he suddenly asked. I looked at him questioningly. "You know, Lucie." He sounded testy. "Whatever you decide, you'll have to have surgery, won't you?" I was a little surprised he'd returned to the subject, given his very definite views, and nodded. "Well, what can I do to help?" He paused, looked down and then back up at me. "I... well... I love you." I sat with my mouth open. "And I want to be there for you..." I certainly wasn't expecting that.

I put my hand on his. "Just be you and love me." Did I really mean that? And why, given the depth of my feelings when we'd stayed at the pub, hadn't I said I loved him too?

We walked home, arm in arm. "You said you wanted me to love you," he murmured as he peeled off my jacket and led me upstairs. I sighed and stretched in anticipation as I reached for him. "No, no. Let me..."

He buried his face in my hair before nibbling my ears and neck, then pushed my arms up as he pulled my sweater up over my head. I held my breath, wondering what he'd do about my bra – he ignored it. "Sit." I did so. He knelt at my feet, pulled off my shoes and socks and started to softly massage my feet and ankles. My feet had always been terribly ticklish so when his fingers brushed my insteps I squeaked, giggled and tried to pull away. He looked up and grinned. "Suck it up sister. You're going to have a foot massage whether you like it or not."

Normally, apart from the occasional treat of a pedicure when I had to hold my breath while the soles of my feet were brushed and scrubbed, I hated my feet being touched.

But this time was different. He reached for a bottle of body lotion I kept on the chest of drawers, rubbed a liberal dollop between both hands and stroked the top of each foot firmly before holding each toe, rubbing in a circular motion and then pulling at them quite firmly. He then moved to my ankles – I positively purred. That done, he stood, pulled me to my feet, undid my trouser button and zip and tugged them down my legs. "Foot up." He tapped my right calf. I obeyed and he tugged the trouser leg over my foot. "Other foot up."

I was now in bra and knickers; he was still fully clothed. I reached for him again and this time was allowed to help him out of his jacket, sweater, shirt and trousers. "Now, you just make yourself really comfortable. I think you're going to like this – quite a lot." I lay back, wriggled into the softness of the duvet and closed my eyes. I expected to feel his weight join me on the bed but no – I felt his hands on my ankles before he massaged his very slow way towards my knees. "Bend your knees now." I did so. "Good girl." His hands kneaded the backs of my knees, my kneecaps which was oddly arousing, and then my lower thighs. By this time, I couldn't stop myself from holding onto the headboard and rocking from side to side, whimpering softly in excitement.

My gasp was audible. He'd pushed my open legs over his shoulders as he pressed his mouth to my pussy through the silk. One hand grasped my left buttock, the other joined his mouth, rubbing and very tenderly pinching me. I could do nothing but surrender to the most amazingly erotic sensations and all too soon was shaken by wave after wave of mindless pleasure shaking my whole body. "Oh... my... God..." was all I could whisper as I shuddered through the final little ripples that slowly faded away.

I heard a chuckle and looked down. Resting his chin on my belly, he smiled up at me and licked his lips. I stared at him and stretched my hands towards him. "I don't think so." He sounded thoughtful. "You said you wanted me to love you. I think you deserve some more – don't you?"

Before I could even take breath to answer, he moved to lie on my right and started to stroke and lightly scratch my midriff, stomach and sides while he softly scraped his teeth on my shoulder. Pulling my rather old, saggy bra down, he held my right breast in both hands, kissed, licked and sucked my nipple, moved to my throat and back again. It was deliciously arousing and, pressing my thighs closely together, I just couldn't stop myself coming again – mellower tremors than my earlier convulsive spasms.

He kissed his way down my still-quivering body, pulled the soaking wet silk to one side and thrust hard. I wrapped my arms and legs around him, pulling him ever closer. Hardly surprisingly, he came within seconds, I was all orgasmed out but delighted in his shaking passion.

I'd been pleasantly surprised that he'd been able to stay, his explanation of booking a couple days off made me feel important and cherished. I made us breakfast and then he left, saying he was needed back in Bath. As I waved him off, I realised that he'd managed to re-entwine himself round my heart but whether it was the phenomenal sex or a much deeper connection, I couldn't quite tell. I had to acknowledge that being admired and loved was very nice indeed and I wasn't about to spoil it by too much analysis.

Anyway, I had an appointment to see Zainab that afternoon and as I walked down the getting-all-too-familiar corridors, found, much to my surprise, I was almost looking forward to my next step.

I felt very calm and composed. "I've been doing a lot of thinking..." Zainab sat back and smiled encouragingly. "Well, I think, on balance, I should opt for a mastectomy." I took a deep breath.

"I think that's a very wise decision Lucie." Zainab sounded warmly approving. "Hopefully the cancer hasn't spread, which should mean conclusively everything will be removed in one fell swoop. And of course, depending on the tests on the removed tissue, there may no need for anything more than a little mop-up radiotherapy. And what do you think about reconstruction?"

"I think not. At least for the moment. But I'd like to keep that option open for a later date. If I can…"

"That's no problem at all, of course you can Lucie." Zainab leaned forward and looked deep in my eyes. "I know what a very hard decision this has been for you. For what it's worth, I think you're absolutely doing the right thing."

"I just want to make sure everything's gone and I'm completely clear before I even think about cosmetic surgery. I mean, if for some reason I do need radiotherapy, well, I don't want it to have to go through a bit of silicone. And if it's not all gone or I need chemotherapy…" My voice cracked a little as the magnitude of what had just been agreed hit me.

We talked a little more before Zainab confirmed I'd receive a letter within the next two weeks, giving me a date for surgery. "You'll probably be in for two or three days. Just til we're happy the wound is healing well. And it really would be better if you're not on your own for another few days after that."

I knew I'd have a warm welcome at Anita and Jeff's again. "That's not a problem Zainab. I'll sort it out."

Another thing I had to sort out was the upcoming holiday with Di. We were meant to leave very soon and as I had no idea when my operation would be, or how long it would be before I could safely travel, opting out seemed the only reasonable thing to do. I called her. She was upset and concerned all at the same time and then very cross I'd not told her sooner. Mixed in with all of this was her cautious pleasure at meeting a new man – it was someone she'd known for some time. They'd actually gone out a few times, but just as friends. It was one night when Di had invited him to her's for dinner that sparks had begun to crackle and they'd not looked back since then. I was delighted for her and knew she'd have a great holiday without me but with him. I promised to keep her updated on my progress. "At this rate I'll be writing a bloody blog," I mock-whinged. It was so good to have so many people who were there for me.

I'd been so preoccupied with me that I'd barely been aware of the news but this was a story much too monumental to be missed. Apparently, there was a virus rampaging through country after country, making many people terribly ill and killing an unprecedented number. It had travelled across the Far and Middle East and was currently raging through Europe. There were cases in North and South America as well. Coronavirus was now classed as an official pandemic, rather like the Spanish Flu in the early nineteen-hundreds when millions had died.

Obviously, it was all very shocking but I couldn't help feeling it wouldn't last, and nor would it affect that many people, me included. How wrong I was.

The first thing that rocked my little world was that within the space of a week, every client emailed me saying that, very regretfully, they had postponed all training and development activities for the foreseeable future. I was stunned – in a heartbeat I'd lost all income. Granted there were a couple of outstanding invoices but those wouldn't last me that long.

Sam rang me towards the end of that disastrous week to share his news. All cafés, bars and restaurants had to close with staff being furloughed, but as he went on to explain, he would continue to work on the gardens at the various locations. "But we can still see each other, can't we?" he'd said. "After all, we know each other, don't we? Won't we be in a bubble?" From what I'd understood, a bubble was the term for a capsule of just a few people so it seemed he could be right.

We talked a little more. "You know, the last time – oh, it must have been about a hundred years ago when there was a pandemic, it lasted about two years." I gasped as the enormity of what he'd just said hit me.

No work for two years – or perhaps longer? How on earth would I cope? And what about Susie? What about my friends? And – not that I wanted to be selfish but even so – what about me? My health? Perhaps even my very survival…

As I read and re-read the letter informing me of the date and time of my surgery, my hand shook. It was now official – barring any unforeseen cancellations, my left breast would be removed in nine days' time. I sat clutching the crumpled sheet of paper for many minutes before placing it on the coffee table, then spent several minutes very carefully trying to smooth away the creases. After that, and even though it was lightly drizzling, I didn't bother with a coat, but walked round the garden umpteen times in an effort to calm down and come to terms with my chosen reality as silent tears rolled down my cheeks, mingling with the rain.

I decided to ask some of my closest local girlfriends over so, the Saturday evening before my due date, seven of us gathered around my table – naturally we kept all the windows open, I couldn't have managed what was to come without that get-together with some of the most important people in my life.

After we'd enjoyed a starter of caramelised onion, spinach and feta filo-pastry tartlets, I served a roasted and sun-dried tomato risotto accompanied by a mixed leaf green salad. We chatted about this and that but over tiramisu and coffee I told everyone what the next few weeks would bring. It was a tremendous relief when everybody said they thought I'd made the right decision. "You know, you're really lucky this is going ahead," Kate had said. That stopped me in my tracks; I hadn't thought about it like that but of course she was right. Our wonderful NHS, whilst preparing for the inevitable surge in demand, was already beginning to buckle under the strain of patients with this new virus. And that would surely mean that non-essential treatments would have to be put on hold. Everyone nodded their agreement and I started to feel much more fortunate and much less of a victim.

Helena volunteered to take me to hospital, Anita said 'my room' would be ready for me whenever wanted and everyone reassured that they'd help as and when they could. The evening ended with hugs and tears all round with more promises of support. Despite the ever-present knot of fear deep in my stomach, I went to bed smiling.

Three days later, a bit too bright and early for my liking, Helena walked with me to my designated room. Bless her, she stayed with me for a couple of hours so we sat in a small conservatory that led off the main ward, overlooking a small carpark.

"This is all very civilised," she remarked as we made ourselves comfortable. We went on to talk about work, films, clothes, shoes – she adored shoes – anything and everything except for what would be happening shortly. We heard the lunch trolley being trundled in at which I sniffed hungrily; breakfast had only been water as I was first on the afternoon's list. Helena glanced at her watch. "Sorry Lucie, I'm going to have to love and leave you." She got to her feet and, making sure no-one was around, hugged me close. "Now, you take care. See you soon." And she was gone.

With a sigh I returned to my bed and, rather than watch other people eating, put in my earphones and started listening to one of my new audio books. I was really getting into it when a very pleasant nurse interrupted me. "Time to get ready." She was much too cheerful for my liking but I dredged up a smile as she drew the curtains around my bed. Minutes later I was gowned and cannula-ed up and shortly afterwards was on a trolley, being wheeled down to theatre. I lay back, breathing deeply, trying to control the panic that was threatening to swamp me. The nurse patted my shoulder reassuringly. "Don't you fret Lucie. She's really good, you know." It was reassuring to know she rated the surgeon but that didn't still my fears. The trolley stopped. "Now Lucie, look at me and start to count." I got to four...

Chapter 9

S o, there I was – lying on a hard bed in the recovery room. The first few seconds were like my usual blissful drowsy moments when reality gently nudges into an increasing consciousness, but all too soon pain and fear kicked in and I had to take a few deep-as-I-could-manage breaths to calm myself. The nurses were very sweet and, urged on by them, I was soon sitting up and sipping a glass of tepid water. After that I slumped down again to doze and this time was allowed to rest.

About an hour later I'd managed to wake up properly and felt well enough to stick my tongue out at a nurse who'd told me I really ought to sit up. She looked surprised, then laughed. "Good to see you back to normal." Whatever my new normal is I muttered to myself as over-riding waves of self-pity swept over me. I then stopped, telling myself not to be so unreasonable. None of this was her fault. In fact, none of it was anyone's fault – it was just bad luck and the sooner I came to terms with that, the better things were likely to be.

I was desperate for a cup of tea but wrinkled my nose at the small cup of tepid pale brown liquid that had been handed to me. She laughed at my obvious distaste. "You can have a proper hot drink a bit later. Don't forget you had a couple of tubes down your throat." I nodded my understanding and obediently drained the cup. Later, I was offered a very small portion of scrambled eggs that had probably been on the food trolley since breakfast but ate them gratefully along with a cup of much hotter tea. I started to feel much more like me.

I'd been told that visitors really weren't allowed so of course hadn't expected to see anyone. It was getting dark and gloomy when I saw Anita's masked face peering through the partially-frosted glass door. Apparently, given the severity of my operation, she'd been given permission to visit. I'd started to feel a little better anyway but seeing her was such a treat, and although I was still croaky, was more than ready to talk. "I'm not going to stay long," she said firmly. "Just thought I'd drop in for a few minutes to make sure you're okay." Her 'few minutes' was actually an hour and a half and though it was lovely to see her, I was relieved to lie back and rest as I watched her close the door behind her. A little later, along with more painkillers, I was offered a sleeping pill which I gladly accepted.

The next morning, I awoke and, for a few moments, couldn't think where I was. As I remembered everything, I raised my hand to touch my left breast to find a flat, hard dressing. No, it hadn't been a dream. It was absolutely real. I couldn't stop myself – I started to cry and even though the act of crying hurt, just couldn't stop. I hadn't realised how heart-broken I'd be to lose something that had been so integrally part of my identity in so many ways.

It was only when one of the lovely nurses came round with medication that I managed to pull myself together. As she handed me the small paper cup, she looked at me sympathetically. "It's just reaction. Most people find the first few days difficult." I nodded. What she didn't know was that my tears had, in large part, been self-recrimination as I'd realised how my mother must have felt when she'd undergone her mastectomy and how I wished I'd been more understanding. I thought I'd done my best to support her but had only been in my early twenties, so how could I have properly grasped the full extent of her suffering?

That night I thought I'd sleep so had refused a sleeping pill. By two thirty in the morning, I was climbing the walls and desperate for a drink, so got out of bed and shuffled my way to the nurses' station. They were very kind, allowing me to sit with them as I enjoyed a really hot cup of tea, before shooing me back to bed where I fell into troubled dozes, punctuated by random dreams of falling down endless flights of stairs or being chased through dark threatening forests by strange outlandish creatures.

I remained in hospital for another day before I was deemed fit enough to be discharged. I was given an appointment to see my consultant in two weeks which was when all the results would be available so any further treatment could be discussed. As I took the letter, I grimaced, hoping beyond hope that none would be needed. Jeff came to collect me and, as I walked outside, was delighted beyond words to be in the warm sunshine.

Two mornings later when I was cautiously washing, was horrified to feel what I could only describe as incredibly sensitive tiny lumps and bumps in my left armpit. Anita rushed me to my GP who, having checked me carefully, declared that all I was suffering from was a post-operative infection. All, I thought? All?! I was almost sick with relief. A rather uncomfortable drain was put in place, a prescription of strong antibiotics given and further appointments planned for the district nurse to visit every day to make sure all was well with the drain were organised. Luckily, everything cleared within a week and, as the drain was removed, I breathed a sigh of relief. Another week of antibiotics was prescribed 'just to mop up any residual infection' which seemed entirely reasonable. I didn't like to mention that the antibiotics made me feel terribly lethargic and under par, a very small price to pay.

But nothing, absolutely nothing had prepared me for the spells of anger, fear, resentment, and grief over losing my breast that continued to engulf me. I managed a semblance of control during the day – it was the nights as I lay in bed tossing and turning when they struck and I shed many bitter tears as quietly as possible, desperate not to disturb my hosts. Sometimes I went downstairs and sat at their kitchen table, staring into the darkness and clutching a hot drink I'd allowed to get cold, while chaotic thoughts raced through my mind.

The next day I felt much more like the old me and said as much to Anita who'd persuaded me to stay a little longer, just to make sure I was strong enough to be on my own. She took me to the supermarket, so I was well stocked with milk, bread and eggs as well as plenty of fruit. Biba had been looked after by Bart and Ed, and was in a surprisingly good mood, coming to greet me as I opened the front door. I stepped in – marvellous though it had been to be so well looked after, it felt wonderful to be back in my own space.

"Good to be home?" Anita knew me so well.

A few minutes after Anita left, there was a knock on the door. When I opened it, all I could see was a huge bunch of flowers with a pair of legs underneath, I recognised the shoes. "Oh, Ed, you shouldn't have..."

Bart followed Ed in and they made me sit down while they fussed Biba, found a vase for the flowers and opened the bottle of fizz that Bart had been carrying. They left after about half-an-hour when it became clear I was flagging. "Now just you shout if you need anything..." was their parting shot.

Anita had insisted on chauffeuring me for my follow-up appointment in a tone I knew all too well – there was no brooking any argument with her. We arrived for the initial treadmill of being weighed, briefly examined and recovery symptoms being noted by a registrar. Eventually we were shown into the consulting room where Zainab sat next to my consultant. Much as I wanted to read their faces, it was impossible because of their masks.

I took a deep breath. She smiled at me; I knew she was smiling because the corners of her eyes were crinkling. "Well, Lucie…" I closed my eyes for a moment to compose myself and dug my nails into the palm of my right hand.

"I'm very glad you made the decision to have a mastectomy. There was one large and two very small tumours that were hidden behind the main one, all quite aggressive. And we've confirmed more than ample margins round all of them so we're as sure as we can be everything's been surgically removed."

My palm was starting to hurt so I relaxed my clenched hand and looked down to see four red crescent marks etched into my flesh.

"However…" I'd never liked 'howevers' and leaned forward slightly.

"Given the margins, we don't think that chemotherapy's necessary…" I could feel a little of the tension leave my body. "But after you've properly healed, we want you to have twenty-one days of radiotherapy here…" She indicated my left underarm. "Just to discourage the possibility of any further tumours in the lymph system." She'd made the cancer sound like a naughty child and I giggled which, I think, surprised her.

As before, it was Zainab who talked me through the details of my further treatment. She said it would take several weeks before the wound and surrounding skin would be strong enough to withstand radiotherapy. "But really, the sooner it can start, the better," she said and I nodded. The leaflet she gave me described possible side-effects and as I glanced through, again remembered how exhausted my mother had been after hers and how thin her skin had become, remaining so for the rest of her life. I shivered.

The clouds had lifted to a bright day so we bought a bottle of prosecco and sat in Anita's garden, toasting to the news being so much better than it might have been. "I know there's more to get through, but it's wonderful you don't have to go through chemotherapy, isn't it?" It so was…

One day, very unexpectedly, Zainab rang me to say she was visiting one of her patients at the local hospice the day after tomorrow and would I like to pop down and see her? I agreed but as I put the phone down, my hand trembled – weren't hospices places where people went to die?

It turned out I couldn't have been more wrong. Hospices were places of respite for people with life-changing conditions. True, some would die because they were approaching what was delicately termed 'end of life', a much gentler way of saying dying, I thought. But there were many people like me, people who were living through a cancer that was very unlikely to kill them – then anyway. This hospice was a vibrant, cheerful place where everyone talked openly and freely about absolutely everything – such a refreshing change to some of the conversations I'd been having where some people had recoiled at the very word 'cancer'.

And I needn't have been so worried. Zainab simply wanted to talk about the possibility of my taking anastrozole on a long-term basis. "It's tamoxifen for older patients," she explained. I looked at her indignantly. "Oh come on Lucie, you're well into your sixties…" She chuckled as she looked into my mock-outraged face. "Clinically speaking, that's hardly young you know. Anyway…" she continued before I could say anything more. "…there's a lot of evidence to suggest that taking it really helps protect patients from future cancers." She handed me yet another leaflet explaining what the drug was and its possible side-effects. She then looked at my scar. "Very good Lucie. Very good. I don't think it'll be too long before you can start your radiotherapy. Just two or maybe three more weeks." She watched me pull on my pale grey poncho, adjust my dark grey scarf adorned with pink hearts and smiled. "And, after the radiotherapy, we'll fit you with a prosthesis. Best to let your skin get over all that before you start to wear one."

We talked a little more before parting. She handed me a month's supply of anastrozole and an A5 printed form. "Take one every morning," she instructed. "Oh, and keep a note of any side-effects. There probably won't be anything but just in case, it's good to know exactly what's happening." She pointed to the piece of paper. "After twenty days, I want you to have a blood test. As soon as I have the results, I'll be in touch – that'll probably only take a day or two. Okay?"

Sam had been texting throughout so it came as no surprise when he asked if I was well enough for a visit. That would be lovely I texted and sat back to plan a menu. It'd been ages since I'd bothered much so the prospect of cooking for someone else was a real tonic.

He opened one of the bottles of chilled prosecco he'd brought along with a huge bunch of lilies, and we smilingly clinked glasses. "You're looking so well," he said with a note of wonder in his voice.

"I feel so much better," I replied. I did too. Apart from a tightness and general tenderness across my left torso, I felt really good.

We'd only kissed cheeks when he arrived but when I moved to hug him, he moved back slightly. "Is this really okay?"

I looked at him. "Of course it is. I've missed you. I'm fine Sam. Really am." I winced very slightly as I raised my left arm a little too quickly. He stood still, looking unsure.

I didn't know what I expected of him. I really didn't know what to expect of myself either but knew I certainly didn't want, or need, to be wrapped in cotton wool. Taking his hand, I walked us into the sitting room, sat on the sofa and patted the seat next to me.

"Sam, it's still me, you know. I've just had surgery and need to recover from that. I'm not going to break if you touch me…" I reached over and held his hand.

He raised his arm and, with a sigh of contentment, I cuddled next to him. We stayed like that for some time until I realised that lunch wasn't going to finish cooking itself.

It felt wonderful, the two of us being in the kitchen together. He made his undeniably excellent bread sauce while I lightly sautéed the vegetables. The chicken was as good as I'd hoped, as was the apple and blackberry crumble I'd prepped the previous day. For some reason I'd not hit the spot with my custard so he quickly cooked more while I mock-sulked – of course his was superb, I admitted through pretend-clenched teeth which made him laugh.

After lunch, we went for a walk but a sudden downpour drove us back and we arrived home cold and soaked through. "I need a hot shower." I dashed upstairs, shedding my thin jacket on the way. I stopped at the top of the stairs and looked down. He was standing by the front door, gazing up at me. "Come on, slowcoach." I quickly stripped off and started to run the shower before peering round the bathroom door to see what he was doing. By this time, he was on the landing but still fully clothed. "I'm freezing. You can join me if you want to." I don't know why I said that but I was damned if I was going to let what little body confidence had left be dented. He didn't join me but sat on the closed loo, watched me and then held out a fluffy towel for me to step into.

He looked deep into my eyes. "I don't want to hurt you. Or embarrass you."

My heart melted as I took his hand. "You won't. But please, please don't ignore me – or it…"

He looked down at my body, raised his hand and then dropped it to his side again.

He sat on the side of the bed, watched as I finished drying myself and pulled a dressing gown over my shoulders. "May I?" He raised his hand. I smiled encouragingly and nodded. His touch was so light, it almost tickled and I giggled which made him chuckle. "Doesn't it hurt?" I could see he was genuinely curious.

"No. It doesn't hurt as such." I paused and thought. "It feels tender. Sensitive. But that'll fade in time." I looked down at myself – the scars were red and slightly raised. I'd not properly looked at myself since the operation and grimaced. "I know it's not pretty but it can only get better…" Ridiculously, tears came into my eyes and I blinked them away impatiently.

"Oh Lucie, sweetheart please don't cry. I'm sorry. I didn't mean to upset you…"

I wound my arm round his neck and pulled him towards me. "Silly. You haven't upset me. I'd so much rather not be like this but it is what it is…" My words were muffled as his mouth found mine. Our kisses were soft and gentle but soon become more ardent and demanding. He softly bit my throat as I lightly ran my fingernails down his spine. He nibbled my lower lip. I pulled at his earlobe with my teeth. I'd have been more than happy to leave it at that but knew he wanted more and, truth to tell, it was pretty wonderful to be fancied at all.

"God, I've missed you so much…" His voice was husky as he pulled me over onto my side. Seconds later I found myself on my hands and knees – his hands gripped my hips as he thrust himself into me, moments later felt him come. He collapsed over my back, panting, before pulling away from me and lying on his back next to me.

It was quite late when we decided we were hungry so went downstairs to nibble on cheese, humus and breadsticks. Sam opened another bottle of wine but after one sip which made me wrinkle my nose, I moved onto diluted orange juice – clearly, I wasn't the great drinking partner he'd first met.

The next morning, I decided to have another salt bath; my mother had taken salt baths to help her wounds heal, saying they really helped so I'd opted to do the same. I think she was right too. He sat on the corner of the bath looking down at me as I gently splashed the warm water over my body. "I'm so nervous that I'll hurt you, and that's the last thing I want to do. You do get that, don't you?" I did.

We'd enjoyed a huge take-away lunch; despite lockdown, the Boathouse had started take-away meals which I'd happily taken advantage of. A lighter meal that evening seemed in order so I flash-fried asparagus, chorizo and halloumi which was accompanied by a bowl of room-temperature bulgur wheat with masses of finely chopped parsley spiked in a fragrant lemon dressing. The oils from the chorizo mingled with the lemony dressing, making it turn a deep pinky-red. Keeping with the lemon theme, I'd prepped two large glasses piled high with lemon posset and even baked some pretty little lemon muffins. It was clear he was suitably impressed.

In bed, I leaned across to kiss him. For a split second it was like kissing a statue but then I felt his lips curving into a smile as he responded. His hand moved down my body to my pussy and as we continued to kiss, he gently fingered me. I pulled my arm back a little so I was holding onto his hardness and was swept back to my younger inexperienced years when feverish snogging and heavy petting was all we dared do. Tongues in each other's mouths, body rocking against body, hands intent on giving as much pleasure as possible – it was electric and as little spasms of pleasure rippled up my body, I bit his lower lip. Moments later he came. We drew back enough to be able to look at each other – hot, sweaty, sticky. Still panting, he grinned – this was no time to be coy – I grinned back.

He left early the next morning and, for the first time, fully embraced me, his chest gently pressed against mine. "See you soon sweetheart," he whispered into my hair. I hugged him back.

A few minutes later I heard a text come through. 'We're a great team in the kitchen and besides that you fuck like an angel. Too good to let go. Sam xx'

Later that morning the phone rang.

"Just what the fuck are you playing at, Mum?"

"Susie? What the hell are you talking about?"

"You know. Not telling me that you've been ill. Still are for all I know. I'm not a kid. How fucking dare you treat me like one?"

I took a deep breath. "How do you know?"

"This morning. I got an email from Di." I heard a couple of clicks. "Listen to this… 'Hi Susie, I've not seen your mum just yet but hope to very soon. She's recuperating from her mastectomy and from what she says is making a great recovery. Luckily, it looks as though she doesn't need to have chemotherapy but almost certainly will have to have a few weeks of…'"

"Okay, Susie. Enough." The realisation I'd been completely wrong in not telling her almost broke my heart and I could feel myself starting to cry.

"Don't cry Mum. That's just not fair. How would you feel if I were ill and didn't tell you? You'd be furious and quite right too." I heard the catch in her voice.

"Susie, I'm so, so sorry. I never meant anything bad. It's just I didn't want to worry you. And you're so far away – of course that's fine but I couldn't find the right way to tell you. And Susie, it all happened so fast. Tests, then surgery, then more surgery, then tablets, then no more tablets…" I paused to wipe my nose. "But I'm getting so much better…" and I went on to tell her exactly what had been happening.

"And that's everything Mum? Sure you're not leaving anything out?"

I winced at the truth of her anxious anger. "Nothing Susie, I swear. And I absolutely promise you, I'll never ever not tell you anything ever again." There was silence. "Susie?"

"Yes Mum. I believe you. Don't you ever, ever do anything like that to me again though. Ever. You hear?"

We went on to talk about what she'd been doing, about Patrizio, what they were planning for the next few weeks, about her work, how I was feeling, how pleased I was to have lost some weight but wished it had been in a less dramatic way – that made us both laugh albeit rather shakily.

"You know Susie, I'm really lucky. I mean, the NHS's waiting lists have had to be frozen – you know, because of Covid? Well, because I was diagnosed before anything had been said or done and because mine wasn't a huge operation, it kind of slid through. Just imagine if I'd been diagnosed now and had to have any treatment put on hold? Now that really would have been scary, wouldn't it?"

When, after another twenty minutes or so, we said our goodbyes we'd both cried. I'd apologised many more times as the full enormity of what I'd done – not done – struck home. I realised how angry, upset and frightened she must have been and was deeply ashamed of myself. Nonetheless we ended with our usual 'love yous' and I knew that in Susie not only was I fortunate enough to have a wonderful daughter but also a dear, dear friend.

That evening while getting ready for bed, I decided to look at myself. Properly look, not the hurried glances I'd limited myself to since my operation. Naked, I stood in front of my bedroom full-length mirror with all the lights on. I took a deep breath and started with my feet – they looked pretty good as I'd recently painted my toenails. Legs – maybe, just maybe, they were a tiny bit thinner? I smiled. Hips and waist – still chunky, but I thought my waist looked a little more defined. Hardly surprising, to a large extent I'd lost my appetite in recent weeks. Reluctantly I shifted my gaze upwards and stared at my chest. My right breast looked forlornly alone against the relative smoothness of my left side. The scar ran from my breastbone horizontally across my chest to under my arm – it was slightly bumpy and red but that, I'd been reassured, would fade in time. I lightly ran my hand over where my breast had been. The whole area was sensitive, the scar especially so. I raised my arm to look at the site of infection – that was tender and seemed very slightly irritated. I dropped my hand and turned away as tears ran down my cheeks before getting into my baggy tee-shirt, getting into bed and pulling the covers over my head.

The next morning, I decided to look again. This is you, I told myself fiercely, you can't pretend it's not. This time I started with my face – that hadn't changed. Same good skin, same greeny-hazel eyes, same wide mouth, same laughter lines when I smiled. Same relatively smooth neck. Same good shoulders. I'd put my hands over my chest – same well-manicured nails. Slowly, I spread my arms. Okay, so I had only one breast. That was the one and only difference. As I took a deep breath, I knew this was the time to make an important decision – I could play the victim, be the sickly woman who'd suffered a mastectomy, unable to come to terms with it – or I could opt to be a fighter, an Amazon who'd elected to undergo a mastectomy in order to deal with a cancer that was potentially threatening her life. In that very heartbeat, I made my choice and as I pulled a soft t-shirt on, winked at my reflection and hummed one of my favourite songs – 'I Will Survive' by the redoubtable Gloria Gaynor.

A couple of days later, I'd just taken my sixteenth anastrozole and was putting the rubbish out, when I felt a sudden rush of heat engulf my whole body. It started in my toes before surging to the top of my head. Bart was outside and must have noticed my knees buckling because he came rushing over.

He wouldn't hear of my not going in so moments later I was settled in their spacious sitting room while they fussed over me. Ed made me tea while Bart made me put my feet up and told Bon-Bon to keep me company which, being a cat, he ignored and stalked off swishing his tail. I stayed with the boys for almost an hour until the feeling of being scared and shaky passed almost as quickly as it had begun. Reluctantly they let me go home but only after I'd promised to call if they could help – as I closed my door, yet again I realised just how lucky I was to have so many people who cared.

That terrible feeling happened again in the afternoon though and this time an overwhelming wave of nausea hit me as well. That night, I suffered the most appalling leg cramps that were impossible to rub away. I knew something was wrong but doggedly continued taking the little white pills, after all Zainab had been quite definite that I should take the medication for three weeks before having a blood test. And, I reasoned, wasn't it worth the odd side-effect if that meant the cancer wouldn't return? Much as I tried to remain upbeat, the symptoms worsened, usually leaving me in floods of tears as my resolve to be stoically brave crumbled a little bit more each time.

Early on the morning of the twentieth day, I went for the required blood test. The following afternoon Zainab texted to ask me to have a consultation with her on Zoom as all health professionals were trying not avoid seeing people face to face. 'It's because I'm not due a visit to the hospice for another couple of weeks' she'd explained, adding there was nothing to worry about. That reassurance didn't stop me having a deeply troubled night, as yet more nightmarish scenarios ran through my head.

Anita offered to come over for the meeting. "It's just to be there for you," she'd said and I'd gladly accepted her offer. To my exasperation with myself, tinged with an overwhelming relief, I needn't have had such a bad night. The blood test clearly showed I lacked the 'right' hormone receptors for the anastrozole to be of any real use so, Zainab said, there was no point in continuing to take it. "It's a pity, but it is the case it doesn't help everyone. And all that hotness and nausea you've been having? They were almost certainly side effects, so you're probably quite pleased to stop, aren't you?" She beamed at me but then looked concerned as I burst into tears.

"It's ok Zainab, honestly. It's just I've been feeling so, so awful…" After a few moments, I managed to control myself thanks to Anita making sympathetic there-there noises.

She smiled understandingly. "As you're here, I'll just have a quick look." I lifted my sweatshirt and moved closer to the screen. "It's healing up remarkably well – should end up as a fine white line. You should be very pleased – you're doing really well…" She'd made it sound like I was a bright student who'd just passed a difficult test. Anita and I giggled; I was giddy with relief and said as much as we closed our call.

Anita grinned at me. "Celebratory drinkies in order I think," she suggested. We toasted each other with weak gin and tonics and spent a very pleasant hour together before she had to leave.

Thoughts about my finances were foremost in my mind when the phone rang a couple of hours later. It was Carrie. "I'm such an idiot," she started to which, of course, I said she wasn't. "Yes I am. There's no work around at the moment, is there? And even if there was, you're not firing on every cylinder, are you?" I ruefully agreed. "Well, why not do what I do? Get a Monday to Friday lodger. It's brilliant. I get paid every Monday evening so get dosh for the week. I have the weekends to myself and company during the week. In fact, this one goes for a run most evenings. And he keeps things neat and tidy. My last one was really messy – this one's a dream…" She went on to say that her current lodger's employer had just taken on another designer who was currently in a bed-and-breakfast but would much prefer to stay in a family situation. Her lodger had mentioned this and she wondered if I might consider letting my spare room to him? I said I'd think about it and put the phone down thoughtfully. It certainly was an option and not one I'd thought of – but sharing my kitchen? I'd always been a bit fussy about my precious pots and pans; I'd have to toughen up on that one.

It only took until the next day to come to the conclusion that Carrie's idea might just work for me.

As we discussed it further, I found myself dithering – this was way out of my comfort zone. As we'd decided that we were in each other's bubble, I'd gone over to hers that evening. "You don't have to say yes," she said reassuringly. "If you don't like him or he doesn't like you…" she paused and giggled. "Mind you, who wouldn't like you?" I play-slapped her hand. "Now, let's make a list of your dos and don'ts – I always do that. It helps me really focus on what's important and means I don't leave anything out if I decide to see them." That was very good advice so we spent half-an-hour compiling my list.

"I hadn't realised just how picky I am," I remarked as I finally put my pen down and looked at the closely-written sheets of paper.

"It's not being picky. It's being sensible. There's no point in agreeing to someone being in your house if they're going to irritate the shit out of you, or vice versa." She was absolutely right of course and I felt relieved that perhaps I wasn't being too exacting in what I wanted from a paying guest.

The very next day Jules called me and explained he'd recently started an eighteen-month contract with Jaguar Land Rover at nearby Gaydon, working on the design and development of a new model. "I have to be in the office at least twice a week, otherwise I'd be working from home," he explained. "If you don't mind my being in the house some days, that'd be great." He sounded really nice so I invited him over that evening. He was slender and dark haired, I guessed him to be in his early-to-mid-forties. There was a slightly sad look in his eyes but when he smiled, his whole face lit up. I learned that he lived in a little village with the almost unpronounceable name of Llangattock Lingoed, a few miles south of the English/Welsh border, very close to the magnificent Brecon Beacons National Park, was married and had three teenage children. He assured me he always returned home at weekends; his children had all sorts of activities they liked their dad to be part of. He said he enjoyed cooking and suggested he might cook for me occasionally. How sweet I thought, before realising that meant he'd probably be using my Le Creuset pans – if he was a half-decent cook, I'd survive that. We seemed to hit it off so it was agreed he'd move in the following Monday evening.

It was only then that he dropped his bombshell. "There's just one more thing I really ought to mention." He was looking very edgy. I nodded encouragingly but nothing could have prepared me for his revelation.

"I… I'm a transvestite…" His voice trailed off as he looked into my surprised face. He stood. "Do you want me to go?"

I closed my mouth. "Don't be silly." I paused. "Would like a drink?" He nodded silently. "You can talk – or not talk – whatever you want – but I promise you it's okay. Why wouldn't it be?"

The look of relief on his face was heart-breaking. There was always a bottle of Bucks Fizz in the fridge so I took it through with two glasses.

After gulping down half a glass he started talking and once started he didn't stop. Although he'd always known he liked the look and feel of women's clothes, it was when he was his mid-teens that he'd ventured into his sister's room and nervously tried on some of her clothes. "It just felt right," he said reflectively. "I loved it. It was the most amazing feeling. It wasn't that I wanted to be a woman, not then anyway. I just liked how it made me feel." He went on to explain that as Jules he felt he had no choice but conform to the male stereotype of being successful at work, being married and being the breadwinner, which meant he was weighed down with concerns and worries about his family and money. "As Julia…" He actually did look a tiny bit like the wonderful Julia Roberts. "I have fewer worries. I kind of see the world from a different perspective. Julia has more fun than Jules, she goes out, she's a bit flirty." He paused for a moment. "She's more emotionally open than Jules. And the more I do it… you know, pass as Julia, the more comfortable I feel."

He moved in the following day.

We talked loads more in the following days and weeks. I learned that Jules had been married for nineteen years and was still deeply in love with his wife. "But I'm not prepared to let go of Julia. I simply can't. And Pam absolutely won't talk about that side of my life – ever." His voice was melancholy. I was sitting on his bed as we talked. He'd said how much he liked me watching him apply makeup which was when his likeness to the redoubtable actress became even more apparent. "I'm so glad Pam's my wife. Apart from being in love with her of course. She keeps me normal, well as normal as I can be. But she says this…" He gestured at his body that was sheathed in an impossibly snug black mini-dress, "is nothing to do with her." He frowned at his reflection. "Hey, pass up that lipstick, will you?"

I smiled as I handed her the soft pink lipstick. "So, Julia…" I was finding it easier and easier to see Julia as somehow separate from Jules. "Do you want to ditch Jules?"

She stopped mid-application and stared at me in the mirror. "It's a bit like being on a train. I have no idea where it'll stop. I'm now thinking of HRT. To make myself more feminine." She frowned as she pursed her lips. "I think that's what Pam's worried about. She's said more than once she doesn't know where I'm going with all this. And that she feels she just doesn't know me any more. But not many people like change, do they?"

That didn't feel entirely fair. "Well, if you didn't tell her about Julia at the very beginning, then she's more than entitled to be pretty cross. I'm sure I'd have been livid." Julia looked startled. "Don't you think relationships need to be based on honesty and respect? Certainly should be anyway. And if she knew something as big as this and hadn't told you before you got married – well, would you think that was acceptable?" I could see Julia was getting annoyed with me. "Look, you have every right to do what you're doing. All I'm saying is that Pam's also got every right to be upset and angry. It's a terrible shame she won't talk about it but if she won't… can't… well…" I shrugged.

"To be honest, I'm terrified she'll turn the kids against me." Julia's voice was muffled as she blotted her lipstick.

That thought hadn't occurred to me. I watched as she carefully pulled on her wig and made final adjustments before turning to face me. "See what I mean?" I did and nodded wordlessly.

Life wasn't easy... for so many of us...

Chapter 10

I was so glad of Jules'/Julia's company during the week but equally loved the weekends on my own or, occasionally, with Sam. As time passed, Jules became more and more open with me so our conversations ranged from clothes and makeup to politics, from the LGBT movement to antique furniture – the last two being his passionate interests. He was an interesting and articulate man – woman – very good company and respectful of my space. All in all, I thanked my lucky stars to have found such an ideal lodger, as well as someone who was fast becoming a good friend.

I, along with probably all of the country, was delighted to hear that lockdown was being eased slowly so it was permissible to gradually restart one's social life. Not only that, cafés and wine bars were to open, albeit with stringent shielding measures in place. This had a huge impact on what I was able to do, I'd missed catching up with friends over a coffee while people watching. Not only that, it made recuperative therapies very much easier.

Along with end-of-life care, I discovered that hospices offered alternative therapies to people with what was called life-changing conditions. It was very clear I wasn't going to die, not yet anyway, but because I was still on the treadmill of post-operative recovery and undergoing treatment, I was offered a few sessions of aromatherapy and/or reiki which I accepted with alacrity.

In fact, Di had qualified as an aromatherapist several years ago and been kind enough to offer a couple of treatments in the past which had been great fun, but nothing I'd taken that seriously.

The aromatherapy sessions given at the hospice felt different somehow and usually brought me to tears which Tiona, one of the therapists, said was a tangible sign they were doing good. I didn't know whether they actually had healing properties, but what I did experience was a deep feeling of calm and peace afterwards. Along with that; somehow, I developed an ability to not only cope, but to embrace my new reality with more enthusiasm and joy than I thought was possible.

Tiona was an energetic, previous art teacher who'd lost her partner to cancer some years previously. That loss had prompted her to explore alternative therapies and now she combined the two into her life. She was tall, slender, wore her grey hair loose just below her shoulders, and dressed like the archetypical hippy in boho-style clothes – a look that suited her and I really admired.

Tiona's reiki treatments were mind-blowing, no other way of putting it. I felt a real heat emanating from her hands as they hovered mere millimetres above my body. Not only that, the feeling of warmth remained for a considerable time afterwards. It seemed like layers of serenity and wellbeing were being heaped onto me and I relished every single moment.

As I became closer to Tiona, I realised the hospice was always on the lookout for extra help. I didn't know what I could contribute but when Tiona told me about David who had now lost the energy to read for himself, I said I'd be delighted to talk with and read to him. He must have been a very good-looking man but was now a real shadow of his former self – skeletally thin and unable to eat or speak due to his cancer attacking the throat and jaw. On a good day he wrote little notes to people, on a bad day he lay still, taking painful shallow breaths. Luckily, my first time with him was on a good day so we communicated well. He shared that he used to live near a farm/animal sanctuary and helped out whenever he had time, loving in particular the horses and one bad-tempered donkey who had a tendency to kick. It was the memories of these interactions with animals he missed the most – that made both of us cry.

I'd imagined that he'd want newspapers or modern novels but no. His yearning was to return to some of his earliest reading so, with much joy as it had been one of childhood favourites, I found myself reading Anna Sewell's Black Beauty.

I'd finished chapter 47 the previous afternoon so, the next day, walked into the hospice with a spring in my step, looking forward reading David the end of the book which is when Black Beauty is sold to a kind master, getting to spend his remaining days in comfort and ease after all too many incidents of hardship and cruelty.

I was devastated to be told that David had died moments before my arrival; probably as I'd been parking the car. I stood at his bedside, clutching the book. It seemed really important, vital in fact, that I finished what we'd started so I sat next to him and read those last two chapters with as much animation and care as I could. I stayed for a few more moments before leaning over him to kiss his still-warm forehead in farewell.

Afterwards, when my huge, wracking sobs had abated, Tiona sat me down with a cup of strong coffee. "You made such a difference to him. He always looked forward to seeing you and loved hearing you read. You mustn't underestimate the joy you brought to him…"

I probably knew it already but here was absolute confirmation that it was the quality of life that truly mattered, not quantity. This insight gave me such comfort and when, later, I stood by his grave, I silently thanked him for his friendship.

There was also the thought that veganism, or at the very least, vegetarianism, was helpful in the healing processes. As an avowed omnivore I didn't really understand this – organic yes of course, but to completely avoid meat and fish? I thought both, probably in moderation, were good in a balanced diet. Tiona said she was giving a talk on the subject one evening, so I decided to go along; good to be open-minded at the very least was my reasoning. There were about half-a-dozen of us and as it was still warm, we decided to sit outside in the hospice's lovely garden. It was all very informal and proved to be much more interesting than I'd imagined. Tiona was adamant that veganism was incredibly good for the body as well as emotional wellbeing, passing round a couple of leaflets on the subject. I knew vegans ate nothing coming from another living being but hadn't realised that included any food that could be seen as exploitative, like honey. We shared recipes which I found fascinating. At half-time we took a break for tea or coffee and some of Tiona's peanut butter cookies. I had to admit they were absolutely delicious. We went on to talk about animal welfare; I was stunned to find how much my own thoughts were in line with Tiona's. As the talk came to a close and we tidied up, was in reflective mood.

My contemplation was broken because as we were leaving, I noticed a colourful poster up in reception and paused to take a closer look. To my amused astonishment there was to be a male strip show in a couple of weeks at a local club, the Cazbar; all proceeds going to the hospice. I turned to one of my fellow-patients. "Hey, I don't suppose you'd like to go to this, would you?"

Jane looked at me and sniffed. "I don't think it's quite me dear, but perhaps you enjoy that sort of thing." I was sure Jane was a good twenty years younger than me. We'd had a few really nice chats but it was clear I'd misjudged her. Apologising for any offence but thinking she might have missed out on a lot of fun in her life, I left.

Bart was in the garden the next day so I went outside for one of our customary over-the-garden-hedge chats when I mentioned the hospice's strip show and Jane's scandalised reaction. "That's such a shame. We're away that weekend, else we'd have come along for a giggle. Oh, and while I think about it, would you look after Bon-Bon for us?" Of course, I was delighted to; I was still missing Whispa terribly and as Biba was a pretty self-sufficient character, found that Bon-Bon's new-found tolerance of my pettings gave much solace. We'd just said our goodbyes when Bart turned back. "Why not ask Jules? He might quite like it."

That evening I recounted the same story to Jules. "I don't suppose Julia would like to come with me?" I really didn't know if I'd overstepped the mark.

He started at me. "Really?"

Julia and I had gone out for strolls and picked up take-away coffees on the way when no-one had blinked an eye except when she'd worn the shortest of short denim skirts, so passing as a woman didn't seem to present a problem.

"Why not?" It seemed a fun idea to me.

"Have you ever been to one of these things before?"

"No. Have you?"

"No. And I'd really like to..."

I chuckled. "Bet we'll almost certainly be the only male strip show virgins in the place, but it'll be a giggle."

As the show was on a Friday, Jules arranged with his wife to get home on the Saturday morning rather than his normal Friday evening.

I really hadn't counted on Julia's overriding preoccupation with dress and makeup. Apart from interminably going on about what she should wear for what seemed like ages, on the actual evening she continued dithering and asking my opinion which she then ignored. In the end I got quite cross with her and, choosing one of her black mini-skirts, black tights, lightweight ankle boots and a sparkly top, told her to stop faffing and get on with it. I'd have been happy enough in jeans but decided to join her in an outfit with more glittery panache. At long last I managed to get us out of the door.

I'd not been to the Cazbar before and, rather gingerly, made my way down the stairs to a large cellar with a long bar along one wall. Normally it would have been crammed with people but due to ongoing restrictions numbers were limited so, thankfully, there was room to move around. The audience was entirely women and, despite Julia's initial nervousness, no-one gave her a second look – except for one woman who glanced admiringly at her everlastingly long legs.

I'd expected to see a small stage but that wasn't the case as I soon found out when the first stripper, dressed as a cowboy, made his way through the crowd. He headed to the bar and as we watched he slowly unbuttoned his very tight checked shirt to cheers and screams that got louder and louder the more he took off, until all he was left with were cowboy boots, his hat and a minute red thong which barely contained his very obvious bulge. As he continued to gyrate, one or two women reached forward to stroke his smooth oiled chest. He reached down to his thong with one hand and, while holding an aerosol of shaving cream with the other, pulled it away to reveal his very large cock, immediately spraying foam all over his shaved pubic area. I didn't know whether to be shocked or titillated but the sight of an almost naked man with shaving foam dripping from his swinging dick made me laugh so much I almost cried. As he made his way back through the crowd, he was very close to Julia who reached down and patted his pert bottom, much to my astonished amusement.

After a pause for us to buy more drinks, the second stripper appeared, dressed as a fireman. "Bit obvious, isn't it?" I whispered to Julia who grinned. This man was older but had the most amazing body which he teasingly displayed as he slowly stripped. He was much more into interaction with the audience and wandered around in his black leather thong, fireman's helmet and boots, lap dancing some of his audience who'd been lucky enough to find a ringside seat on the few tables around the wall. I thanked my lucky stars I was standing as I didn't think I'd have coped with an all but naked male bottom, albeit very well waxed and oiled, in quite such close proximity. Eventually he made his way back to the bar and amidst encouraging shouts and whistles, pulled away his thong. My mouth fell open – I'd never seen such an enormous cock.

"Fair makes your eyes water, doesn't it?" Somebody's comment could be clearly heard, many of us laughed.

As I watched him cover his nakedness with shaving foam and swing himself from side to side, the foam spattered onto the nearest onlookers and it suddenly struck me just how unsexy it all was.

After an interval where a few nibbles were served and more drinks bought, the younger stripper reappeared, this time dressed as a gladiator and the same routine followed; this time with more audience participation. I stood back a bit but Julia was more than happy to join in, holding his belt and slowly pulling it away from him to encouraging shouts from the rest of us.

The final act of the night was the older man who came out dressed in white just like Richard Gere in An Officer and a Gentleman. Now that, I thought, was more like it and, for the first time that evening, gleefully felt myself get caught up in the moment. When he passed close to me having removed his jacket, I reached out to brush my fingertips over his smooth glistening shoulder. His thong was white which turned blue under the ultra-violet spotlight, making his tanned skin look even darker, and when he eventually stripped it away, there was a collective gasp. He seemed even bigger than before and this time when he used the foam, there were even more appreciative screams and applause.

As he left the bar, we all clapped loudly. The last act was the best and I said as much to Julia as we stood at the bar to get another drink. "They were very well endowed, weren't they?" They were too.

Julia chuckled. "Elastic bands." I raised my eyebrows. "Oh, don't be silly Lucie. They use elastic bands to make sure they remain… impressive."

"Well, the last act was certainly… impressive."

We giggled our way home where we had a nightcap and a very long chat. It was clear that Julia's confidence had soared. "It's the first time I've felt truly accepted." She was almost in tears.

"Everyone was too busy having a good time, weren't they? Why wouldn't they take you as a woman? Even if you do tend to overdo the makeup..." She did too.

I was so tired, I had to go to bed and left Julia downstairs, listening to Fleetwood Mac and playing with the cat. She looked more relaxed than I'd ever seen her.

After I'd waved Jules goodbye the following morning, I strolled into the garden with my customary cup of tea. I still wasn't used to being accompanied by just the one feline friend and was sadly standing by Whispa's rose, taking in the heady scent, when I heard Ed's voice.

"It was such fun," I said in answer to his question about how we enjoyed the evening, and went on to tell him all about it. I was still giggling about Julia's fixation about what to wear before realising that he wasn't reacting in an Ed-type way. "Anything wrong?" He was misty-eyed. "Come on over and let's have a chat..." Naturally I'd always counted Bart and Ed as being in my 'bubble' so we'd been in almost constant contact.

Two minutes later he was standing in my kitchen while I made him a strong coffee with a brandy on the side. We settled ourselves back in the garden. "Bart gone shopping?" Ed shook his head and then told me the whole story.

Many years ago, back in the days when family expectations were heterosexually high, Bart had married Jackie. Two children and a long time later he realised it had not been the right thing to do but apart from infrequent forays into gay bars when he'd picked up the occasional man, he'd tried hard to maintain his marriage – mainly for the sake of the children it had to be said.

It had taken Jackie's second affair to finally lead to a divorce that was sadly acrimonious. Bart adored his children and ensured he maintained, at the very least, a good working relationship with his ex.

That trauma had taken its toll. Bart had convinced himself that he wouldn't find another permanent relationship so had been content enough to continue cruising gay bars and that, along with putting his energies into his work, had kept him fully occupied.

It was during a touring production of Macbeth that he met Ed. There had been an instant attraction and the rest, as they would have said, was history. They married the following year and, apart from the normal odd matrimonial spat, had been joyfully happy ever since.

However, about three years ago, Jackie had been diagnosed with Parkinson's disease and Bart, ever wanting to alleviate the burdens on his children, been very helpful in putting up a few disability aids to help her around the house. Right from the very beginning, Jackie had never completely accepted Ed but it was at this time that her veiled dislike became out-and-out hostility, even over the phone.

She had been getting much more forgetful and difficult of late which was making life difficult for everyone who was trying help. After much pressure from her children, she'd agreed to undergo tests only to have early-onset Alzheimer's confirmed. It became increasingly clear that she couldn't cope on her own for much longer so Bart had spent more and more time staying with her, helping look after her, sorting out finances, and putting the house on the market which of course meant massive decluttering. At the same time, he'd managed to find a very nice nursing home near their daughter.

"And that's not the problem – I understand. He's really helping the kids out and that's fine. But it's so not okay that I'm sidelined all the time, even when he's here he's kind of not – know what I mean?" I nodded. "He's focused on her all the time. That's all he talks about. It doesn't feel like we're close any more..." I wondered if he meant just sex. "And frankly I'm getting pissed off..." He paused to wipe his nose on his red silk handkerchief, "...and anxious. Really scared that all this is making him go off me..."

I had to stop him there. "You two are the archetypal old married couple – you know that." Ed didn't smile back. "This is a crisis Ed. A crisis about a woman who's sick and only going to get worse. In her lucid moments she's probably terrified. Who else can sort out all the practicalities in her life? All his hands-on concern will come to an end because once she settled into this nursing home, he'll just be making the odd visit." Ed's tears were still flowing. "Haven't you guys talked about this?"

"Not much." Ed's voice was muffled as he blew his nose.

I knew that great gay marriages were much rarer than straight, even though there were fewer divorces in that community. I knew that many gay men felt insecure in their relationships, long or short term. And I knew that with two people, both fuelled with testosterone, sex was high on the list of must-haves. And now that Bart was spending longer and longer periods of time away, a cornerstone of their relationship was being left wanting – small wonder that Ed was distraught.

"But you talk all the time – don't you?" Ed was still sniffling. "Look, if you don't tell Bart exactly what you're thinking and feeling, how's he meant to know? It's not crystal balls he's got in his pants, you know." That made him smile. "It's all very well being able to talk about sex – you do talk about sex, don't you?" Ed giggled. "That's the easy bit, just getting naked. Anyone can do that. It's getting emotionally naked that's important…" I thought of Alex who'd relished our emotional nakedness and of Richard who hadn't. "Talk to him. Tell him that you're nervous about the time he's away from you. Tell him you feel sidelined. Tell him you're anxious about Jackie being so anti-you, that you don't understand it and, more importantly, that you don't like it. Tell him you want… no, need, to feel a part of this in some way. Tell him you admire what he's doing and how you know that if, God forbid, you're ever ill, you know he'd be there just the way you'd be there for him. And tell him how much you love and value him."

Bart returned three days later and when I saw them in the garden the following day, I could tell they'd talked. Bart looked relaxed and Ed was positively glowing. As we said our usual hellos, I raised a quizzical eyebrow at Ed who silently winked – I knew that now they were on an even better road…

It was the following weekend that Sam came over, saying it had been far too long since we'd been together. Whilst it had been lovely to chat on the phone, as I saw him walk towards me, I realised just how much I'd missed him. No doubt about it, there was a powerful physical attraction between us; given my fluctuating wellbeing I found it surprising – maybe it really was love?

He kissed me. A gentle, tender kiss. "I've missed you so much."

He brought a large carrier bag in which there were the makings of a sumptuous meal. That was so kind of him, and I didn't like to say that I too had been exercising my culinary mind when going shopping the previous day. With a stifled sigh, I put a couple of the bags I'd bought from the fridge into the freezer.

Any slight resentment I might have felt disappeared as he was cooking and then served up the most scrumptious meal. We started with tiny chicken meatballs served with a garlicky yoghurt sauce on a bed of watercress. The pepperiness of the watercress combined with the softness of the meatballs and coolness of the dressing was perfect – I said as much. He beamed. "It's one of our new recipes – so glad you like it."

There was more to come. He whipped up a large platter of moules à la marinière accompanied by French bread – another triumph albeit a messy one.

I adored mussels but always ended up with creamy sauce all over my hands as well as dribbling down my chin – to me, cutlery was totally redundant for a dish like this. Luckily, he was almost as bad.

I'd watched him make tiramisu, again one of my favourites provided the coffee wasn't too strong, which it wasn't; I knew because I'd insisted that I make it. "Just excuse me a moment…" And with that he disappeared.

I sat alone for a few moments before hearing his footsteps coming downstairs, sitting in stunned amazement as he rejoined me. He was completely naked apart from my Cath Kidson blue flowery apron.

"Well, you said how much you enjoyed the strip show last weekend, so I just wanted to see what you thought of this." He gave a very creditable swirl.

I shook my head in disbelief. "This just for me?"

"All for my dear" I saw the front of the apron twitch slightly and felt the stirrings of my own arousal.

The tiramisu was, of course, delicious. As I swirled my finger round the glass to lick up every last bit of the soft cream he smiled. "Coffee?"

"Please. I'll have a green capsule please." Very recently I'd found a 'pre-loved' Nespresso coffee maker on a local social media page and been unable to resist it. I'd been trying a different colour capsule every time I fancied a coffee which made the whole process much more fun.

He must have been quite hot because his naked skin had kind of stuck to the wooden chair so peeling himself off it was a bit of a struggle. I started to laugh at his expression of discomfort and found the more I laughed the more I had to laugh. Tears were running down my cheeks and my face actually hurt; every time I looked at him somehow that started me off again. Eventually, I subsided into the occasional hiccupping giggle.

"You done now?" I nodded before chuckling again. "It wasn't that funny…"

I hiccupped again, desperately trying to stifle the residual laughs that were threatening to break free.

That laughter continued for the next day or so – everything we said or did triggered giggles from me which, I think, started to wear a bit thin for him. I certainly couldn't blame him for that and apologised more than once. "Guess it's like a release from everything that's been happening," I tried to explain whereupon he nodded but I could tell he wasn't convinced.

What was wonderful was that he still seemed to fancy me, uni-breasted or not. However, more often than not, he opted for doggy style – so he didn't have to look at my front I'd assumed, and that made me feel a bit less sexy and a bit less loved. But equally, I realised it was still a relatively new relationship and it was a lot for him to take on board. And, I reasoned, I'd probably feel much the same were the tables turned – and it was with this rather disheartening thought that I waved him goodbye on Sunday afternoon…

Chapter 11

My consultant was very pleased with the way my wounds were healing, she used the word 'satisfied' but her smile told me she was way more than satisfied. Upon hearing those words, I couldn't resist a giggle, that made her smile wider. She was usually quite straight-faced so seeing that was a real plus and made me feel like I'd just passed an exam – that made me laugh too.

Her 'satisfaction' on my progress was such that the following Monday found me sitting in the waiting room of the radiotherapy area for my first session, with Anita by my side. Looking around was a very sobering experience, many of the other patients were obviously very poorly which drove out my feelings of self-pity. I had no idea what to expect but everyone was so kind and welcoming that my nervous butterflies soon disappeared. I was shown into a large treatment room dominated by a huge machine which looked pretty intimidating but was affectionately introduced as 'The Zapper'. I was told I'd have to be given a tiny tattoo so that every treatment hit exactly the right spot. "May I have a ladybird, please?" The radiographer smiled politely whereupon I realised she'd probably heard much the same from nearly every patient. "Sorry…" I peered at her name badge. "Debbie."

"It does stop being funny after one hears it a hundred times or so," she remarked as she carefully lined up the machine. I turned my head to look at her. "No Lucie, it's important that you stay absolutely still. Getting this mark in the right place could mean the difference between a long-term clean bill of health or not." I returned to the position I'd been told to assume and breathed as shallowly as I could in an effort to remain as motionless as possible. After what seemed like ages but can only have been a matter of seconds, I felt Debbie's hand on my shoulder. "Good girl. You can relax now." I breathed normally again. I was delighted when she brought over a mirror to show me my new tattoo. It was a tiny blue dot just to the right of my left armpit, nothing at all dramatic but it did make me feel like I'd just been initiated into rather an exclusive club.

It took another few minutes for the machine to be lined up to my approximate specifications before I was invited to again lie down on the hard surface. I was moved several times to ensure the rays would hit the precise spot until finally it was judged that everything was in the right place – the rest of me included. "Lucie, we're leaving you now but I'll be in there…" She indicated a small room with a large window facing The Zapper. "You'll be in view all the time. If you need anything, anything at all, just raise this hand…" She touched my right hand. "It'll only take a few moments. Just stay as still as you possibly can."

I closed my eyes and concentrated hard, desperately wanting to feel I was playing a part in my own treatment. I had no idea how long I lay on the unyielding surface but it certainly wasn't long. Debbie reappeared and gently patted my shoulder. "All done Lucie. Well done. See you tomorrow." And with the assurance my subsequent appointments would be much shorter, I left.

Anita insisted we celebrated my first treatment. "Only fourteen more to go now," she said cheerfully as she pulled into the car park of a nearby garden centre. My offer to fill her fuel tank had been refused so I was delighted to see a beautiful little bay tree in a pretty pot I thought she'd really like and, when she nipped to the loo, bought it, asking the cashier if it could be taken out to Anita's car. We enjoyed an excellent cup of coffee and an even better slice of carrot cake, had a quick look around at some of the lovely things on offer, and went outside. "You really shouldn't have," she said as we struggled to fit it into the car but, with a bit of pushing, shoving and a dash of bad language, eventually we managed it.

Although my wounds had healed sufficiently for me to be deemed fit enough to drive, I'd been advised not to for the journeys to and from my radiotherapy. "People react differently to these treatments," Zainab had explained. "You might have no side effects at all but then again you might. Better to be safe than sorry." She'd then given me a prescription for a heavy-duty antiseptic cream specifically for tender skin undergoing radiotherapy. "Use it even if you don't think you need to," was her advice. Ever wanting to play my part, I made sure I did.

The next three weeks passed very slowly. I continued to see many other patients in the waiting room. There was a middle-aged man who'd suffered from jaw cancer with much of his lower face missing, a woman who I learned had three young children who was in the latter stages of pancreatic cancer, a much older man making a slow recovery from prostate cancer, and many, many more. Every day I thanked my lucky stars for small mercies, and strengthened my resolve to be appreciative, to never forget this experience and to make the most of each and every day left to me.

Bless them – Anita, Helena, Shona and Ed took it in turns to drive me for all the rest of my treatments. It came as a huge shock to became as tired as I did, and by the time I reached the start of the third week I was painfully aware I was totally incapable of concentrating enough to drive safely. And although I applied the gunky cream religiously, it didn't stop the area from developing tiny little pin-point burns. I wore the softest t-shirts possible but even they chafed my tender skin and I often woke in tears because I was hot and in pain. As Debbie said on my penultimate session, being grateful for being less ill than others didn't necessarily alleviate distress and discomfort.

I didn't see Sam during my radiotherapy but we talked a lot. When I told him about the little blue dot I now sported, he laughed. "So Lucie, if you're not going for reconstruction, have you thought about getting a tattoo?"

"No, I'd not thought about that at all." I paused for a moment. "I do love yours – you know the dragonflies in a circle? I might have a think about it…"

And I did, off and on, for the next few weeks…

It was towards the end of the first full week after my radiotherapy had finished when, standing under the shower, I realised the patch under my arm was much less tender. I looked at myself in the mirror – most of the little specs of burn had vanished and the whole area felt smoother. For the first time, massaging the gunky cream into my skin didn't hurt as much so, with much caution, I dared to feel the beginnings of real recovery.

I saw my consultant the following week who, after a scan and careful physical examination, said she was very happy to say I was steadily improving. "You'll need regular check-ups of course, but the initial signs are good. I think you're nearly ready to be measured for your prosthesis – Zainab will make an appointment for you. And you can drive as soon as you want…" That was the news I'd been longing to hear; I couldn't stop myself from clapping my hands together silently.

Leaving the sharp antiseptic smell behind me and feeling the light rain in my face was, without doubt, one of the most joyful moments of my life.

Getting into Helena's car, I was beaming in delight. At long last I'd been given the go-ahead to get on with being able to drive, with work (if I could find any), with life – I couldn't wait.

A major benefit of my recovery was that I now felt better able to look outside myself, to be concerned with other people's lives and less concerned with my own. Increasingly I found I'd listen more and talk less as my focus shifted. I much preferred this mindset; it made me feel much more like my old self and even worthwhile – or perhaps I was just naturally nosy I said to myself. I'd then reflected on my recent conversation with Ed; I knew I'd sparked off an in-depth tête-à-tête, prompting them to sort things out sooner than later, all they needed was love and understanding and they had that in bucketloads.

I was at the supermarket doing my weekly shop when I thought the figure ahead of me looked vaguely familiar. As he stopped to pick up some honey from the shelf, I saw I was right – it was Tim, Val's husband. "Tim? It is you, isn't you?" The man half-turned. "How nice to see you. How are you?" He turned round completely; to my surprise he was sporting a black eye. "Goodness me, what have you done to yourself?"

He smiled in an embarrassed way. "Oh, I was in the garage and slipped – hit my head on the door frame, stupid of me... Anyway, how are you, Lucie? What have you been doing?" It was obvious he didn't want to talk about it.

We stood and chatted for a few moments but he seemed ill at ease and keen to get away. I told him I was keeping my fingers crossed about the possibility of more work and he explained that he was working from home more and more. "I think Val finds that a bit tiresome, she prefers having the house to herself during the week." His laugh sounded a bit of a shaky – or was that my imagination? We said our goodbyes and as I watched him push his trolley away, I wondered if it was just my fanciful thought or had he sounded frightened as well as unhappy? I finished off my shopping with that disturbing thought in my head which wouldn't go away.

Anita and I had been in each other's 'bubbles' for the whole of lockdown so now it had been relaxed, I was an even more frequent visitor. The day after I'd seen Tim, I rang to see if they might be putting the kettle on. Obligingly they were, so five minutes later I was at their kitchen table, telling them about our chance encounter. "Of course it might have been an accident. Or perhaps they play games…" Jeff chuckled at Anita's blank look. "Don't pretend you don't know." Very sweetly, she blushed.

So, at first my impressions were dismissed but the more we talked about it, the more possible it seemed.

"Val's always worn the pants, hasn't she?" Anita was the least judgemental person I knew so to hear her taking this seriously made both Jeff and I stop teasing her.

Jeff's face, normally crinkled with smiles, looked sombre. "I must admit, I've been wondering why I'd not seen him." Jeff was a sociable man and, before lockdown, had met a handful of friends for a drink most weeks; Tim had been on the periphery of the group but always seemed to enjoy his time when he did join them. "Come to think of it, he's not come on any of our walks either." I raised an interrogative eyebrow. "Well, we've substituted walks for the pub. I've asked him several times to come along –– he's always made some sort of excuse so I've stopped asking. Hmmm..."

The three of us went on to discuss both physical and emotionally abusive relationships although we agreed that the two often went hand-in-hand. It hadn't been something I'd spent much time considering so when Jeff said that whilst he absolutely agreed that abuse towards anyone – man, woman or child – was completely unacceptable, it was probably harder for a man to seek help than anyone else. "After all, there are still double standards. Everyone feels sympathy for abused women and kids so speaking out is easier..." Both Anita and I started to protest. "No, no, it's true. I'm not saying that challenging abuse is easy – it's just much more socially acceptable for women to do so. Women do sometimes fight back but society frowns on men doing that. Most men have it drummed into them told that hitting a woman is wrong, and it is of course, but the truth is that many men would feel they were less of a man if they're putting up with being victimised." Food for thought Anita and I agreed as we hugged goodbye.

Jeff's comments had bothered me so, on and off, Tim was on my mind. A few days later I decided to call Val. We chatted about this and that for a few minutes and then, after a few heavy hints from me, Val invited me for a socially-distanced coffee in her large garden. "That'd be lovely Val. It's been far too long since we've got together."

I'd known Val for some time, our children had gone to the same Saturday music club where we'd contributed cookies to fund-raise. We'd never become friends as such, more close acquaintances. She was a very tall woman, pushing six feet, and never had that great a fashion follower, tending to what she said was a 'classic' look and, rather cattily, I'd called sensibly ordinary.

Tim had always had far more style and flair than her. He was at least four inches shorter than her with auburn hair and green eyes. He must have been very good looking in his youth, but now looked tired and careworn. His hair was faded, streaked with grey and poorly cut, and he had dark circles under his eyes. One of his signatures was that he wore fabulous shoes, I'd always admired men who wore good shoes but I'd noticed in the supermarket that they were not as highly polished as they used to be. His usual style was a rather country look of checked shirts and tweedy jackets but on the day I'd bumped into him, he'd been wearing jeans and a faded blue sweatshirt, looking much more a shadow of his former smart self.

They did have a lovely garden. We sat by the central feature of a rockery with three small interlinked pools and a tinkling fountain that kept the water aerated for the fish. On our way through, Val had asked, told more like, Tim to make coffee and bring it out to us.

A few minutes later the coffee hadn't arrived. "Hurry up Tim." She turned to me. "You wouldn't think making a cup of coffee would take him so long, would you?" I smiled neutrally whilst inside I was squirming with embarrassment.

Very shortly afterwards Tim came out bearing a tray. His hand shook slightly as put one of the mugs down which spilled a little of the hot liquid over the plate of biscuits. "Oh, for heaven's sake Tim – you're absolutely hopeless. Go on, get back to your work."

Muttering apologies for his clumsiness, he turned to go but not before I'd noticed a small round burn near his wrist on his left hand. Of course, I couldn't be sure but, as a previous smoker, it looked suspiciously like a cigarette burn. There was something amiss, I was much surer of it now.

Val and I continued to chat, mainly about our children. I became aware of a phone ringing and then Tim appeared with a handset in his outstretched hand. "Val…" She glared at him. "I'm so sorry to disturb you dear, but it's for you. It's important, otherwise I wouldn't have bothered…" I could have sworn he looked really nervous, scared almost.

Val huffed and puffed as she got to her feet. "Oh, it's the bank. Excuse me, Lucie. It's probably nothing that my useless husband couldn't have dealt with but I'd better take this in the kitchen. Won't be long…" We both watched her plod down the garden.

As soon as the back door closed behind her, I looked up at Tim who was standing near me, looking very uncomfortable. He returned my gaze and gave a forced smile. "You know old Val…"

I couldn't bear it. "Tim – my dear, are you alright?" His eyes glistened. "I can see what's happening – well, what I think is happening. And I just want to say that

I'm here when... if... you want. I know that Jeff's been really worried about you. Why don't you give him a call?"

Tears came into his eyes. "She's been under a lot of stress recently... she doesn't mean it..."

In a pig's ear she doesn't mean it, I thought. I was desperate to confront her as soon as she came back, but knew that would almost certainly make things worse so I remained as polite as I could. I didn't see Tim when I left shortly afterwards, assuring Val we'd get together again soon.

Half an hour later I was with Anita and Jeff, telling them everything. It was his final remark, 'she doesn't mean it' that was the clincher for me. "We must do something. Mustn't we?"

Jeff shook his head. "All we can do is be there for him when... if he decides to talk."

Over the ensuing days and weeks, several of Tim's friends called or texted him, assuring him of their support, offering a sympathetic ear and a bolthole if needed. Most were ignored, the rest getting a terse text saying that he was busy.

We were all left standing by... waiting... hoping... to hear from him. We didn't but at least we hoped he knew that come the day he decided to reach out, we'd be there for him.

Despite being distracted from myself by other people, the feeling of being lopsided continued to worry and bother me so I was delighted when my appointment to be fitted for a silicon prosthesis came through. I had to admit I looked a whole heap better but quickly found that wearing it made me feel very hot and terribly sweaty. I wore it when going out but as soon as I came home, couldn't wait to rip off my bra and throw the prosthesis on the bed. One particularly muggy day when attending a Zoom call about standardisation of practice and documentation for a college, a leftover from previous work, I had no option than to excuse myself for a moment, leave the room and take the prosthesis out of my bra so spent the rest of the meeting huddled over my papers with my arms folded. I cried when I'd logged off, contemplating a life either under baggy tops or enduring a sticky lump of silicone for the rest of my life.

"It was awful Julia, just awful," I hiccupped that evening when she came downstairs, dressed to kill for an evening out with a fellow t-girl she'd recently met. "I never thought I'd feel quite so bad about this. I know it's only a breast and I'm really lucky to be okay but I hate the way I look…"

She patted my shoulder and made reassuringly there-there noises, patiently waiting until my sobs had quietened to the odd gulp. "Just wait a minute." She suddenly disappeared and then returned holding a silk scarf. "It's only little but let's try it." I looked at her blankly. "Where's your bra? Oh, for goodness sake…" She looked exasperated as I feebly got to my feet. "I'll go…" She disappeared again and this time came back holding one of my older bras between thumb and forefinger. "Don't tell me you actually wear this…"

"Cheeky moo," I muttered as, at her insistence, I pulled off my tee-shirt and put on the off-white bra.

"Now…" She scrumpled up the scarf and gently pushed it into the empty cup. "How does that feel?"

I looked at her, then down at myself. The scarf was, as she'd rightly said, far too small but the principle was there. The silk felt cool and smooth against my skin and I could see that, given more fabric, I'd look okay especially if my clothes weren't too tight. Probably better than okay I thought and smiled at her gratefully. I'd never have dreamt of doing anything like this in front of Jules, but with Julia it all seemed perfectly natural and acceptable.

The following Monday evening, Jules came in with a pretty carrier bag which, a little diffidently, he presented to me. Inside were two huge square Italian silk scarves that I happily used from then on instead of the silicon. My outline certainly didn't look quite as sleek as when I'd worn the prosthesis but, as I felt so much more comfortable, that translated into a new-found body confidence that made me smile.

A few days later Julia and I went out for a drink and were joined by one of her t-girlfriends, Camila. Talk turned to health and beauty.

"A friend of mine had a double mastectomy," Camila was explaining, "and her cancer nurse suggested knitted tits."

"Really?" Involuntarily I touched my silk breast.

"Mmmm…" Camila was busily looking at her phone. "Look."

She passed me her mobile and I scrolled down to see that she was quite right. A company called theknittedboobco sold small, medium and large knitted breasts, all of which sold for well under £20.

"Oh, do let me get you one…" Camila grabbed her phone back. "Now sweetie, what size shall we get?"

After much debate and laughter, they decided that I should try one medium in baby blue with a dark blue nipple and a large one in pale lilac with an imperial purple nipple. That evening was just like when Sam had got stuck to the chair – I couldn't stop laughing and by the end of the evening my face positively ached.

The knitted boobs were in fact a great success. They, along with the silk scarves gave me options, so wearing a bra wasn't the trauma I'd allowed it to become, and as I increasingly felt better about myself, my strut started to return.

That strut really did make a huge impact on my sense of wellbeing. So much so that when I went to see Zainab for a follow-up appointment, I could tell that, for a split second, she barely recognised me. She examined me and confirmed everything was continuing to heal very well. "It's only going to get better and better of course." She went on to congratulate me on finding alternatives to the silicone prosthesis and then broached another subject. "Have you had any more thoughts on reconstruction, Lucie?"

"Thought I didn't have to make a decision yet." I was very surprised, slightly wrong-footed.

"No, you don't. I was just wondering. This Covid thing is already draining some of our services and frankly we all suspect things are only going to get worse over the coming months. It's just if you were keen, I'd be suggesting sooner rather than later, otherwise it might have to be much later."

Promising to give the matter more thought, I left in a reflective mood. It seemed that recovery was a bumpier road than I'd expected…

Chapter 12

L ife, as it inevitably does, rumbled on. I continued to heal well. My energy levels were on the rise almost daily. I started to enjoy walks down by the river where I'd feed the eager ducks and swans, watching more active souls boating on the water. There was still no definite work on the horizon which was worrying but, on an ex-colleague's advice, I was becoming ever more confident on Zoom and Teams so was on the hunt for different, remote ways of working; not exactly my comfort zone, but I was determined to at least give it a go.

Sam had been kept fairly busy with gardens at the various pubs. 'I think if they look well-tended and inviting, we'll be more memorable than other places and people might be more likely to come back to us' he'd said and I'd completely agreed with him. This meant that we saw less of each other which was a pity.

However, he did manage to find a couple of free days and I was more than happy to agree to him coming over. He arrived for lunch when I made one of his favourites, goat's cheese and rocket risotto accompanied by a crunchy, garlicky salad which was followed by some of the tiny cupcakes he'd made for us. He'd brought a real tasting sample of pina colada, chocolate orange, pear and salted caramel, and tiramisu – each more scrumptious than the one before.

Almost inevitably we ended up in bed that afternoon. Usually there was an almost feverish impatience when we hadn't seen each other for a while but this time was deliciously different. We spent ages languorously kissing, fondling, stroking, nibbling until it was me who was trembling in impatient anticipation. Even once locked together, the pace continued to be long and slow, almost lazy, which left me feeling positively boneless with pleasure. There was no doubt about it, sex with Sam was almost as good as it had been with Alex, and that really was saying something.

We showered together which continued the bliss. He rubbed his wet hands down my back, over my hips and then knelt under the stream of hot water to sponge my legs and feet. When, as he stood, I ran my soapy hands down his body, his arousal became very evident. With a quizzically raised eyebrow and a small mock-sigh, I sank to my knees. I heard his sharp intake of breath as his spread legs tensed slightly, and felt his hands in my hair. I'd never given a blowjob under cascades of hot water before and although I found it oddly exciting, for some reason I was overcome by a fit of giggles so by the time he came, we both were laughing uncontrollably. It was a wonderfully intimate moment, followed by more mutual washing and rinsing down. When we'd made quite sure each of us was squeaky-clean, we wrapped each other in big baths towels.

I sat on the bed and watched him dress. "Shall we get an Indian takeaway for dinner?"

I nodded my happy agreement. "There's a takeaway menu in the kitchen. Why don't you have a look while I get dressed?" Smilingly, he dropped a kiss on the top of my head and went downstairs.

I was almost ready when I heard his voice floating upstairs. "Lucie… Lucie?" I went to the top of the stairs. "Be a love and bring my phone down, will you?"

I picked up his mobile from the bedside table; the movement made the screen light up. Going into someone else's phone was something I'd never do, but I could hardly avoid seeing the first two lines of text 'Wow, last night was a-maz-ing!! Can't wait til…'. There was obviously more but that's all that was visible. I stood stock-still and stared at it, unable to believe my eyes.

Ignoring my first instinct to leap in and scream at him, I made my unhurried way downstairs. I was astonished that I couldn't decide how I felt – there were so many conflicting emotions rushing through me. Richard's infidelity was back in my head with a pounding vengeance but, I told myself firmly, I had to listen to what Sam said. I really couldn't think what else this could be other than a message from some woman but I might, just might, be proved wrong.

He was sitting at the dining table, scanning the takeaway menu and looked up with a warm smile. "Oh, great. Thanks honey…" He held out his hand.

I held the phone in front of his face. "What's this Sam?"

As he took the phone from my hand, the screen brightened again. He didn't read the whole message, just what I'd seen. He didn't look guilty in the least but I could see from his stiffened shoulders that he wasn't feeling entirely comfortable.

"Oh, come on Lucie…" He gave one of his most charming smiles. I sat silently, waiting. "It's nothing… well, it's only April. You know? I think you've met her, she's just one of the barmaids at the Mare…"

I blinked and took a deep breath, asking the question I didn't want to but knowing I had to. "Did you sleep with her last night?"

"Well… yes."

A random sense of 'no wonder he was okay to take his time in bed' crashed into my head, before amazement at his calmness kicked in along with a good splash of anger and disappointment. "You slept with her? How could you? I mean, I thought we were something special…"

"We are, for sure we are – but look Lucie, it's not like we're exclusive, is it? I mean we never actually said that." He was now looking genuinely confused.

I shook my head in bewilderment. "No… no… no… This isn't… I mean, I'd assumed that we were an item, especially after you actually said you loved me…"

He cut in. "Well, yes. And I meant it. But clearly you made an assumption and you really shouldn't have done that, should you? Did we ever say we'd not see anyone else? No, we didn't…" To my puzzlement he was sounding annoyed – but wasn't I the injured person here, I said to myself?

At least he was prepared to talk. The bottom line, which I found almost impossible to agree with, was that he saw absolutely nothing wrong in what he'd done.

"Unless you actually say a relationship's exclusive, then it isn't." This explanation wasn't an excuse as far as he was concerned, he really believed this was the case. It gradually sunk in that we had very different expectations on what was or wasn't acceptable in a relationship; I was completely taken aback when he said he was surprised that I hadn't been seeing anyone else when he wasn't around. And the truth was, he was quite right – the minute we'd gone to bed I'd made an assumption that neither of us would sleep with anyone else, in my obviously old-fashioned mind that didn't need actually saying. But much as I really tried to see his point of view, I couldn't; it just didn't fit in with my way of thinking.

The argument, chat he called it, rumbled on, pausing only while he ordered a takeaway – evidently food was still on his mind. When it arrived, he tucked in with relish – it was clear his appetite hadn't been dented whereas I was only able to pick at a few morsels.

When we'd finished, he leaned back, patting his stomach and sighing contentedly. I had no idea why but found that incredibly irritating. "Look Lucie, I think you need to think about all this…" He paused and looked at me intently. "To be honest…" I allowed myself to hope that my point of view had been taken seriously and held my breath. "I think you're lovely, I really do. We've had some great times together so why spoil it? I think it's perfect just the way it is…" I exhaled with a disheartened whoosh. We sat in silence for a few moments. "Look here, why don't I push off now and give you a bit of space – time for you to think. The ball's in your court – you know that I'd love to go on seeing you, but really now it's got to be up to you…"

I was engulfed in a bear-hug before he held my chin and kissed me. I found myself automatically responding but when I felt his mouth curving into a smile, pulled away. I couldn't bear the thought that he might be laughing at me.

He remained cheerfully upbeat as he said goodbye. "Please say we'll go on seeing each other – we're so good together…" was his parting shot. That at least made me feel better about myself than the last time a man had walked out on me.

Over the next few days, I swung wildly from one emotion to the other. I ditched the anger very quickly – after all he'd been kind of honest in his behaviour and certainly transparently candid in his explanations. I did wonder if he'd ever have told me about his… I wasn't sure whether to call them dalliances or something more serious. I also ditched the feeling of being a failure, as I remembered his last words which had seemed sincerely genuine. What was left was a sense of being let-down, along with a sharp sensation of disillusionment and disappointment. There was also a question buzzing round in my mind – I was sure I'd heard the name 'April' before but try as I might I couldn't, for the life of me, think when or where. But mainly I was puzzled. Was I really so out of step with modern thinking?

There was nothing for it – whenever I had a crisis, I had to talk with friends. Everyone of my age-ish agreed with me; that once you sleep with someone, it was reasonable enough to make an assumption that they were not sleeping with anyone else. That was a huge source of comfort to me.

However, one day when I was at Anita's, her daughter Rosie called. As their brief conversation drew to a close, I asked if I could have a quick word. What she said astounded me and, irritatingly, absolutely endorsed what Sam had said – that the new norm was that unless it had been explicitly discussed and agreed, then what I called 'cheating' wasn't infidelity, it was 'fair game'. Clearly such lines had blurred while I wasn't looking!

Whilst I had to acknowledge we hadn't had that 'let's not sleep with anyone else' conversation, for me having to be explicit that I expected someone I was shagging to keep their dick in their pants wasn't something I felt needed to be said. I didn't care what the modern parlance was, being with someone who had such very different values was unlikely to work for me.

I called him that evening. "That's a real shame," he sounded a little sad. "I like you an awful lot and we're really good, but I'm not prepared to be totally exclusive – that's just not what I do… or how I want to operate."

"That's ok. You've got to do what you want – and so have I. It's been a real blast but sorry, it's just not something I want to continue."

"Okay Lucie, if that's how you feel. Good luck…"
And the phone went dead.

He was right, it was a shame but I knew that, for me, it was absolutely the right thing. Nobody however charming, and no sex, no matter how good, was worth relinquishing how I thought a meaningful relationship should be conducted.

It rather shocked me that when I put the phone down, I started to cry. It wasn't because of Sam. I was crying because it seemed all but impossible to meet someone decent who shared my approach to life. And I went on crying because, remembering Alex, I still desperately missed him.

After I was all cried out, I made myself a strong coffee and poured a generous slug of brandy in. As I sat hugging my little black cat who really wasn't in the mood for cuddles but was gracious enough to put up with me and sipped the reviving drink, I resolved that in future only to consider a relationship, full or part-time, where I'd be their 'Number One' and they'd be mine. Memories of Richard's indignant justifications about seeing Kath when I imagined dunking his faithless cock in a bucket of bleach popped into my head which made me giggle the rest of the day away.

Susie called the next day. When I told her what had happened, she commiserated with me but then assured me that what he said was in line with current thinking. "So Mum, this was all about him and not about you, you do know that, don't you?" Bless her, she always knew what to say to make me feel better.

"Anyway Susie, there's something I want to ask you to do for me…"

Sam's question of 'was I going to have a tattoo' had been preoccupying me for some time. At first, I'd dismissed it out of hand – have a tatt at my age? Ridiculous…

But then, rather cautiously I floated the idea to some of my friends and, to my surprise, more were in favour of that than of reconstruction. "You could always have it lasered off if you do eventually decide to go for the op," was Carrie's practical contribution, as had been Di's.

So, when Susie called, it seemed like the ideal opportunity to ask her. "Oh brilliant, you go for it Mum." I could tell she thought it was a tremendous idea.

"And I was wondering if you'd design…"

I was interrupted with squeaks of delight. We talked some more, eventually agreeing that she would have a think and send me some ideas. "Can't wait to get started. It's going to be so cool."

Two days later I received an email from her with a few designs. There were two that caught my eye were an elegant phoenix rising from a bed of flames, and a dragon breathing fire and smoke. After much debate with myself I decided on the dragon but wanted it to be less fierce.

Before emailing her with my choice, I went for a walk down by the river where I sat and watched some children feeding the birds. There was one I particularly noticed – a swan that was slower than the others, probably older or perhaps had been hurt in some way. Recognising the effects of life taking its toll, I smiled.

Once home, I emailed Susie who set to again and came up with a swan with a drooping wing 'swimming' on dandelions; I remembered that, as a little child, I'd loved to blow on dandelion seedheads and watch them float away. 'They're spreading your wishes,' my father had told me with a gentle smile, of course I'd believed him.

Susie's design was perfect so, before I lost my nerve, I googled for a local tattooist.

Three days later I was lying on a surprisingly comfortable couch while Luke, a dark-haired, rather intense, much-pierced and tattooed young man pressed a paper design on my skin as a guide for the actual inking. It took us two sessions – the first to get the outline done, by the end of which I was in tears, having yelped and sworn my way through the entire process. I couldn't believe quite how much it hurt, even though Luke reassured me that the ribcage was one of the most sensitive areas for this so I wasn't being a total wuss. "Take a couple of painkillers an hour before the next session," he suggested as he wrapped clingfilm round me and gave me a small pot of bepanthen cream, this to encourage the skin to heal. I followed his instructions to the letter and the following week was back to have shading and the most wonderful, slightly surreal, watercolours added. Knowing what to expect helped as did the painkillers so, much to Luke's amused relief, I was marginally better behaved.

The end result was nothing short of spectacular and I loved it. "You'll be back," was Jake's parting shot as we hugged goodbye; lockdown had been all but totally lifted and I'd been missing hugs. And after all I reasoned, what was some random bug going to do to me that cancer hadn't?

Once everything had healed and my skin had lost its redness, it looked even better. I wanted to show it off as much as possible – and did – but knew that it would be a long time before I'd be tempted to get back on that couch again. The whole process had been life-changing but far too painful to repeat.

Chapter 13

A group of us had decided to take full advantage of bars and restaurants being open to get together every week or so for a meal in one of Stratford's excellent restaurants. It was an opportunity to eat good food, avoid the preparation and washing up, and have regular catchups. Tonight was to be a curry night at Hussains, a well-respected Indian restaurant on the high street.

Unusually and much to Biba's pleasure, I'd spent the day in the garden and was very hot and dirty. It had been a productive day and the garden was looking much neater.

I took a long shower, luxuriating in the hot water cascading over me. I'd been growing out my fringe and was trying to look less like a Shetland pony so styled my hair with care. Ever the girlie-girl, I was wondering what to wear as I applied my eyeshadow. As I delved into the makeup bag for my lipstick, I came across a box of false eyelashes I'd bought for a laugh when out shopping with Anita months ago. I looked at them reflectively for a moment, then gently peeled them out. I'd not lost my touch from way back – they stuck on perfectly first time. I giggled as I looked at myself. "Looking good there Lucie." I fluttered my eyelashes, wondering whether they were a tad over the top and should I take them off, when I heard a knock at the door.

Pulling on my pink satiny dressing gown I ran downstairs to open the front door and, standing there looking quite nervous was… Richard. As ever he was wearing a smart suit, I noticed he was wearing a silk tie which I'd bought him several years ago. His hair was a little thinner but all in all he looked remarkably dapper, his usual fragrance wafted into my nose. My heart was pounding but somehow, I managed to hold on to as neutral an expression as possible.

I didn't ask him in. I just stood in the doorway… waiting.

He shuffled his feet and cleared his throat. "Lucie…" I said nothing. He cleared his throat again. "I… I'm not with Kathy any more – the whole thing was a dreadful mistake. It's you I want, it's you I need…" His voice faded away as I continued standing, gazing at him impassively. Truth to tell, I couldn't think of a single thing to say and as I stared at him, I wondered if those were the words he'd said to Kathy after he'd dumped me.

He shifted his shiny grey shoes and glanced away for a moment. "Look, you probably need some time. Perhaps I shouldn't have just turned up like this." He looked at me and again I kept my face as inscrutable as possible. "I've booked in at the Arden Hotel – you know, that hotel down by the theatre?"

For the first time I reacted by nodding that yes, I did indeed know the Arden Hotel. "Why don't you join me for dinner this evening? I managed to get a last-minute cancellation at Salt, that place that's recently got its first Michelin star – we could talk more then." Did he think that was going to impress me? "Oh, and I've booked a double room – perhaps you'd like to stay with me? Just like the old days?" He grinned at me, the smile that had so often melted my heart.

He moved closer and leaned in to kiss me, I turned my head so he ended up kissing my ear rather than my mouth. He stepped back. "Yes… well… I'll leave you to get dressed – unless you want me to help you?" He gave me that grin again.

Silently shaking my head, I deliberately loosened the grip on my dressing gown so the top fell open enough to expose my left side. His grin widened as his eyes flicked down but he then froze, taking in the flatness of my chest adorned by that glorious tattoo; I knew he hated tattoos and had said more than once that really bright people never had them. I was delighted to allow him a glimpse of mine. Slowly, he looked up at my face. "What… what happened?" His blue eyes were wide but I couldn't read the emotion behind them.

I gathered the dressing gown together again. "I had a mastectomy." My voice sounded toneless, even to me.

"I… I didn't know… I mean, why didn't you tell me?"

I blinked. "And why would I have done that? We were over – you said we were done." I paused while he shifted his feet again; I couldn't tell whether he was sad, distressed, or offended. "So, I'll join you at Salts about seven thirty. That okay?" I knew the girls wouldn't mind once I'd explained why I wouldn't be with them.

As he half-turned to leave, the thought of how the evening might go was gradually crystalising.

A couple of steps away he turned to look back. "I have to say you're looking good Lucie. Even though you've had that... that operation. Very, very good..." I gave a tight smile as I watched him walk away.

The minute he disappeared I bolted inside, shaking. I rang Carrie who, thank God, picked up. She listened as I poured out what had just happened. "I've said I'll have dinner with him. What do you think?" Although she too was going out for a curry, coincidentally at Hussain's, with another group of friends later, she agreed to come over for a quick coffee.

By the time she arrived more questions than answers were swirling round and round in my mind. Did I believe that he and Kath were really over? If that was true, did I feel even the smallest vestige of sympathy for him? Was I still attracted to him? Did I want him back?

I took a deep breath. "You know Carrie, it was a real jolt seeing him. You know, he still looks really good; fabulous clothes, a sharp haircut..."

She snorted. "Oh... so, he spent a bit of time on making himself look good for you, did he?"

"Oh, come on Carrie. That's not very fair..."

"Fair? Fair! Don't you talk to me about fair. Was it fair the way he left? Was it fair the way he..." I held up my hands in surrender. "Ok Lucie…" She stared at me meaningfully. "You know I'm always here for you and I'll always back you whatever you decide but please, please don't you dare think for even half a second about having him back. He's like a fucking leopard – never ever going to change his spots. He dumped you because you didn't have enough money, that's why he was with her – you know that. And I bet it was her who'd had enough of him. Well, if that was the case, good on her I say." She took another sip of coffee. "Just remember how bad he made you feel so often."

She stayed for a little longer until I said I had a dinner date to get ready for. As we hugged goodbye, she made me promise to get in touch the minute I could. I smiled inscrutably.

I then called Anita, one of the girls going for a curry and told her what had happened. "I've agreed to meet him but may not stay for the whole meal…" Anita laughed. "Tell you what, I'll try to join you for coffee a bit later. Will you guys still be at Hussain's?" We all loved Hussain's, it boasted a wonderfully wide menu.

"Yes, of course we will. And we'll wait for you so if you're not going to come, please call me otherwise I'll be really worried. Now look, don't you dare weaken. If you start to get too jittery or indecisive, just remember how you felt when he left. We'll be thinking of you – good luck…"

It took a little while to get ready, I wanted to look my very best. After much trying on, I decided on a new black, grey and white shift dress I'd recently treated myself to which, teamed with pearl earrings and two long strings of pearls, was transformed into a great evening look. And because heels always made me feel powerful, I wore a black patent pair I'd had for years, they'd always been amazingly comfortable. A red and black scarf and red clutch bag completed the look. A light dust of powder, reapplied lipstick – I was done. I checked myself out in the mirror, nodded and smiled – I looked pretty dam' good and knowing that gave me a much-needed boost of poised self-assurance.

He was sitting in the tiny reception area and stood as I walked towards him. He looked me up and down. "You look… stunning." I smiled my thanks and, sidestepping his kiss, sat. "Let's celebrate getting back together." A glass of prosecco was waiting for me – not champagne I noted.

We talked – actually he talked. He said how much he'd missed me, how it was fear of hurting me even more that had stopped him from getting in touch with me, and how much he now wanted me. He went on to say he knew he'd treated me badly and had felt terrible about it – apparently, it had cost him many sleepless nights. "I've thought about you almost every day," he added. Only 'almost' I thought, after five years wasn't I worth a bit more than that?

I nodded and smiled as I sipped my drink. He offered me another but I refused saying I wanted a clear head. He grinned again. Bet he thinks you're finding it difficult to resist him, the little voice in my head whispered. You just wait and see I whispered back.

Salt had a semi-open kitchen on the ground floor with tables arranged in clusters they called 'rooms'. There were several more 'rooms' on the first floor which was where we were guided to. I sighed inwardly – hadn't he remembered my love of all things culinary and that dining with a view of the kitchen would have been my idea of heaven? We made ourselves comfortable at the beautifully laid table. "Lucie, this is a special evening. You must order whatever you want." How extraordinary I thought; he'd never said anything like that before, not that he'd ever begrudged spending his money on a good meal.

Smiling sweetly, I scanned the menu. I ignored the actual items on offer – unlike anything I'd ever done before, I was going for the most expensive dishes I could find. When the waiter came for our order, I asked for scallops on a bed of crumbled black pudding followed by chateaubriand with a lobster tail.

In answer to his, "What would you like to drink?" I asked for Laurent-Perrier's pink champagne.

The scallops were superb, I thoroughly enjoyed them. Halfway through my dish, I leaned across to taste of his pork terrine knowing full well how much he'd always disliked sharing. He said nothing but it was very clear from his tightened jaw he'd much rather I hadn't done so.

He wanted to know all about my mastectomy but I dodged that by telling him about my volunteering time at the hospice. "That was very good of you," was his response to my enthusiasm.

He went on to talk more, saying we should take more trips, mentioning places he knew had been on my bucket list with him. From a modest day at Kew Gardens we'd never done even though I'd mentioned it several times, to a Mediterranean cruise to revisit childhood memories of when we'd lived in Malta, from wandering down the renowned Grafton Street in Dublin that I'd enthusiastically read about to revisiting Marseilles which had been my last holiday with Alex – all fairly modest stuff it had seemed to me, and had been crushed when all my suggestions had been brushed aside, my irregular work and tight budget being given as excuses. "That sounds lovely Richard, really lovely," I said at his every suggestion. As the minutes passed, I could see him relaxing more and more.

Our empty plates were cleared away and more champagne poured. He continued talking about future trips but this time I really wasn't listening. I was waiting for the sound of our waiter bringing up our main courses.

He was now in the middle of explaining just what he'd missed about me which was all too obviously meant to make me feel special but actually didn't. I smiled and nodded in all the right places but deep down knew that in his eyes, at very best, I was his second if not third choice. Fleetingly I wondered why he'd come back, suspecting an emotional weariness, what he thought would probably be an easy option, and a bit of a power trip being the reasons. But he wanted to come back, so did I really care why?

I heard footsteps, then saw our waiter at the top of the stairs.

Now was the time.

Taking a deep breath, I leaned forward and took his hands in mine, the first real physical contact we'd made.

"Richard... my dear..." He met my eyes and smiled. "You have no idea how much I was desperate to hear from you after you left. How hard it was for me to function. How many nights I cried. How angry I was – and at the same time how rubbish I felt and how long it took me to get over it." I paused. "You know, no-one had ever, ever treated me quite so badly." As he took a breath, I put my forefinger against his mouth to stop him. "And now, out of the blue, you just turn up. You say you've left Kathy? Well, that may or may not be true. You say you want me back?" Out of the corner of my eye I could see our waiter, laden with a large tray, getting closer. "Well sweetheart..." The waiter was now only two or three steps away and well in earshot. I squeezed Richard's hands. "The truth of the matter is I'm nothing like the woman you so unceremoniously walked out on." The waiter was now at the table. "To quote you my darling – this... is... just... not... good... enough..." I let go of Richard's hands and leaned back as the dishes were laid out by the now-embarrassed waiter – Richard's look of stunned astonishment was slowly replaced by anger as my words started to sink in.

As the last dish was placed, I stood up. "Enjoy your dinner Richard but I won't join you. As you well know, enough really is enough. Goodbye." And with that I picked up my floaty red and black scarf, slung it over my shoulder and turned away. Much as seeing his reaction would have made my small retaliation even more perfect, I made sure I didn't look back.

The sound of my high heels resounding as I strode away from Salt made me tingle with empowered pleasure. Head held high I made my way towards Hussain's, where I knew my dear friends would be waiting. At that very moment, life really could not have been sweeter...

Vivien was the only child of Oscar and Susan Heim, sharing her mother's birthday on 9 October 1947, born in London.

Due to her father's posting to Malta, the family spent the early part of her childhood there, returning to London in the mid-1950s. Married at 24 and after what she called 'an awful lot of faffing about', Vivien decided to pursue a career in education which proved to be a turning point in her life as it became clear this was the working love of her life. The untimely death of her mother in 1976 came as a huge shock, a sorrow that came back to haunt her when she suffered the same disease many years later. Vivien's only daughter, Harriet, arrived in 1988. The years between 1995 and 2001 took their toll; following the all to early death of a dear friend and her father within days of each other, the ending of her marriage, redundancy from the teaching job she highly valued, and battling breast cancer – life was hard. In order to support herself and her daughter, Vivien seized every opportunity that materialised – from taking in lodgers to share their home, to teaching, assessing vocational qualifications, teaching English as a foreign language, training, management consultancy, and life coaching. She has even been an official wedding registrar!

It was mainly through the support network of her friends that she survived all this head held high; a group of women (and the occasional man) who hold strong and true to each other to this day.

As she felt she needed to concentrate on her daughter at least until she had left school, Vivien was in her mid/late 50s, having shied away from it entirely for over a decade, before she ventured into the world of online dating. These dalliances left her fearful, exposed and self-conscious, yet excited, comforted, and courageous. It was those feelings that inspired this, her first novel – *Enough Really Is Enough*.

Lightning Source UK Ltd.
Milton Keynes UK
UKHW030654021122
411507UK00001B/124